SASQUATCH, BABY!

BETHANY BROWNING

ALSO BY BETHANY BROWNING

WAR OF THE WILLS
Watch now on Amazon Prime Video!
On the brink of financial ruin, William Hadeon III gets a lifeline in the form of an inheritance from the grandfather he never knew. The only problem? He must outlast his scheming father in a war of wills to claim what's his.

Coming Soon
DEAD SPREAD
When tarot card reader Carrie Dettwiler stumbles across the mayor's dead body, everyone's convinced she and her rescue raven Waggery have performed a deadly dark ritual. Determined to divine who's behind the murder, Carrie must rely on her knowledge of the town's secret history to reveal the killer.

Coming Soon
QUEEN OF TENTACLES
When Mariner's Cove fortune teller Baba Caracatiță turns up dead, only one person in town has a motive—rival tarot card reader Carrie Dettwiler.

Coming Soon
TROUBLE'S AFOOT
A Hollywood icon goes missing, and the only clue is a foot in one of her shoes that washes up on a Malibu beach. But the foot doesn't match her DNA.

Read her short stories and horror novellas, get extras for this book, and more at bethanybrowning.com.

For the liars, bad friends, and try-hards—and the people who love us anyway.

CONTENTS

I DIDN'T GIVE a good goddamn that the house was in a fire zone. The entire state of California was a fire zone. Between the live-laugh-love crowd setting off explosives for gender reveals, rednecks tossing lit cigarettes out of their F-150s, and actual arsonists setting fires ON PURPOSE, it was only a matter of time before the Golden State was a smoldering ruin, a charred remnant, a seething cadaver of smoke and brimstone.

Because I'd probably be dead within six months anyway, why not indulge my fantasy of a Nancy Meyers kitchen, zero neighbors, and all-encompassing silence? If the area around my new house ignited, burning me with it, well, dems the breaks. I'd already failed at killing myself once so far. Let nature have a crack at it. I'll raise a glass of chardonnay to the flames from my soaking tub while falling ashes cascade around me like snow.

"You win, inferno," I'll scream at the embers. "Lash me to ashes."

My stupid realtor, Annie, was sanguine about my fire-related questions. "The previous owners understood the risks and applied fire-hardening measures," she said.

"That sounds like something. What's that mean, exactly?"

"Flame-resistant building materials, accessibility to water for spot fires, roof sprinklers, clearing around the home," she said. "Look, I'm not saying the house can't burn down. It can. But they did as well as anyone could to make sure it doesn't."

"But it could if someone wanted it to?" I asked.

"You—you *want* the house to burn down?"

"Only if I'm in it," I said. "Otherwise, I guess not. I'll take it."

"Um—"

"Lighten up, Annie. I'm joking. Transferring the funds today."

My new home was in Del Norte County halfway up a mountain behind a town called Fort Dick. If I'd had any friends left, I'd have loved to joke about that. I tried out some material with the cashier at the Fort Dick market, but his name was Dick, too, and he seemed wildly unimpressed with the tiny, shaved-headed woman in Tom Ford sunnies, swinging a Kelly bag who said she was, "Seeking Fort Dick. And maybe some armory balls?"

"That'll be $762.43," he said, not breaking eye contact or flinching.

"Wow," I said. "Pricey for a small town."

"It's all about the supply chain," he said. "Plus, you've got four cases of chardonnay here, three cartons of American Spirit yellows and sixteen boxes of Cheez-Its—among other things."

I'd miscalculated. That wasn't going to be enough.

"You know what, Dick? Let's add one more case, two more cartons, and four handles of Smirnoff, m'kay?"

"You say so," he said. He took his time gathering my new items while I looked around the shop. The only things that distinguished this dump from every other shitty mercantile I'd ever been in was the sheer volume of bigfoot merch: Fuzzy keychains. Bumper stickers that said *Gone Squatchin'*. A display of laminated *Sasquatch Hunting Permits*.

I rolled my eyes and wished I had a phone to distract myself.

"This is enough to kill a person," Dick said as he added the items to my bill.

"Great Zeus willing," I said. And when he looked concerned: "Laughter is my love language."

He stood there, his jaw slack.

I snapped at him. "Hello? Anyone home?"

"Silence is my love language," he said.

"Good one, Dick. Is that short for *Dickathon*?"

Silence.

"Joking," I said. "I know it's a nickname for *Dickthaniel*."

"Here's your new total," he said, pointing his stubby finger at the green digits.

"I feel judged," I said to Dick, as I pulled out my credit card.

"No, ma'am," he said. "What you do is your business. That's how we see it out here. We stay out of your shenanigans; you stay out of ours."

I looked at the credit card machine, which had a handwritten sticky note on it that read "Insert chip into bottom."

I had to bite my tongue about that one.

"Thanks," I said. "This is gonna take a couple of trips. Be right back."

"You a tourist, or you move here?" Dick asked as I fumbled my way into and out of the store, loading my car up with the supplies. He followed me back and forth but didn't offer to help carry.

"New neighbor," I said. "Name's Tabitha Eggs. Most recently of the Napa Valley, but that lilting accent you hear is from my heritage home in the heart of South Cackalacky."

"Ah, yes. You bought the Casa de Crypto," he said. "Heard about you."

"You mean Casa de Cryptid?" I asked, motioning toward a particularly garish bigfoot-themed display where he was wearing a Smokey Bear hat.

"Good one," he said. "But no. The owners did some funny-money scheme. Bitchain or CrossFit or one of those."

"Right," I said, scooping the cartons of cigarettes into my arms like beloved infants.

He continued: "House built by people with more cash than sense. Had the place only a year before they went bust. They decamped under the cover of darkness to who-knows-where. And now there's you. A lady who tells bad jokes and likes wearing her hair very, very short."

I laughed. "Not sure I 'like' wearing my hair in this style, Dick. And you can tell all the gossips that I'm changing the name of the house. Officially. Right now."

"What're you calling it?"

I thought for a moment.

"Kevin."

"What, now?"

"The house's name is Kevin."

Dick seemed frozen in his spot for a moment. I saw his tongue dart out between his lips. Then:

"You up there alone?"

The only correct way to answer this question, ladies, is no. Even if being smothered by a townie would make your death plan a whole lot simpler.

"No," I lied. "Not alone."

"Good. You shouldn't be up there alone."

"Bears?" I asked.

"Something like that," he said. "Don't wander around in the dark." He handed me a card. "Call old Dick if you and your—"

"Bodyguard. Former Mossad agent. Name's Krav Maga."

"Where's he now?" Dick was squinting like he was trying to focus.

"That's the thing," I said. "You won't see him until it's too late. And then he'll be the last thing you see."

"Your, well, whatever," Dick continued, with a dismissive wave of his hand. "Call old Dick if you need anything. "'Specially during fire season, you hear?"

"Thanks," I said. "We'll be fine."

He looked pained, like he was struggling to not talk.

"Everything OK?" I asked. I closed the trunk on my C-class with that satisfying, German-engineered "whunk" sound.

"You be careful is all."

"You know what they say about a creature with big feet?" I asked.

"What do they say?" he asked.

"Big shoes."

He shook his head and shuffled through the doors of his market, setting off that little bing-bong sound as he went.

"Love language, Dick," I called after.

I sat in my car for a moment to collect my thoughts. My former friend Abby would have told me not everything needed to be a joke and that I should use my wit to make people feel good about themselves, not to trick or tease.

"It's mean, what you do, sometimes," she once said.

I wondered about that. How mean could it be if everyone laughed? I was giving the people what they wanted, wasn't I? I was still confused as to how my life had gotten so thoroughly demolished. If I'd been less funny, would I be sitting here in the parking lot of a general store in the back of beyond, planning to drink myself to death?

The drive here had been long, but the journey that landed me here—in a forest outpost with no friends and armed with nothing but terrible humor and a raging alcohol problem—had been grueling.

A small taste of the life I'd dreamed of, far from prying eyes that would judge me, is all I was concerned with now. And if the forest, or something in the forest, slaughtered me before I could end it myself, then that would be one more blessing I received and didn't deserve.

CHAPTER
TWO

PHASE one of my plan was called Fall Off the Face of the Earth, and it continued apace. I'd already changed my phone number, shut down all social media accounts, and skipped out of the Napa Valley and my fancy wine country friends without a single good-bye. I was now standing inside my ideal final hermitage after christening it with an evocative and accurate name (Kevin), stocked up on groceries, wine, and smokes, which meant that I was ready to enter phase two: Getting Settled.

I piloted my car up the vertiginous switchbacks to 10101 Tule Elk Way, where Kevin awaited. I realized why Dick said folks around here stock up on supplies. Driving on this pockmarked and shredded ribbon of road was a major undertaking, and it wasn't even the snowy season.

The scenery was breathtaking—if you're into that sort of thing.

Trees loomed like skyscrapers. Ferns with ladylike fronds, old as dinosaurs, flourished on every ridge in a shade of bright green that was nearly neon. A kaleidoscope of ten thousand shades of green.

Nature and I weren't well acquainted. Other than the few places I liked to go drinking with friends, I didn't venture too far out into the wilderness. While I was drooling over photos of the interior of the house, I hadn't given much thought to the forest part of it.

Dangers await in forests, don't they? The light's not right. The air's too still. Shadows become obstructed by all the living and dying things that move through them. Is that a light breeze or an ancient ghost? What is that smell, at once so fresh and clean but with hints of rot, spoilage, decay? Hidden holes that hungrily snap at ankles. Branches that fall from three stories high. Fungi that can shut down organs. Plants that poison with one brush of the hand.

Creatures with hot breath, slavering mouths, claws for rending flesh.

I needed this forest to destroy what was left of my will to live, and it was already doing a bang-up job.

I'd only ever lived around people. In neighborhoods, boarding school, college dorms, the Victorian I shared with the girls before they all got lives and left me behind.

I thought about what my former friend Norah would have said about my new living situation. Probably something along the lines of, "It's great for a vacay, totally 'grammable, but where's the shopping?"

Serena would swoon and start thinking of ways to monetize. "Airbnb," she'd say. "Maybe small weddings or pop-up dinners with famous chefs." She was always full of ideas.

Abby would line every shelf with bottles, potions, candles, and other good-smelling things.

I put them out of my mind. They'd never see this.

The house itself looked exactly like the photos. My stupid realtor, Annie, whom I'd never met in person, had let herself in earlier to turn on the heat and some of the lights. The sellers had been eager, I was told. I'd requested they leave their furniture and housewares, which they did. The house itself, lit from the inside, looked like a glittering jewel set in a lush green velvet case.

A lush green velvet case full of secrets.

"This is the last place I'll ever live," I said with an involuntary shudder, as I hoisted the first case of chardonnay over the thresh-old. "Let's make this good, Kevin."

Before I went back outside to get the rest of my groceries and luggage, I found the corkscrew, poured myself a tall glass of wine, and slugged it back in three greedy gulps. The first one for Norah, who never had a criticism of me she didn't vocalize. The second for Serena, who used me and my money for years, and when she found a man who was willing to support her, cast me aside. And the third for Abby, who, with her perfect life, perfect local hand-crafted business, and overall perfect perfection, could go suck an artisan-woven seagrass basket full of donkey dongs.

CHAPTER
THREE

I IMAGINED a flurry of activity upon arriving here, but the truth was there wasn't much to do. The former owners had left all their stuff. Why bother unpacking when these two weirdos left me a closet full of clothes?

The closet was clearly designed by a woman who also mistakenly thought she'd need designer clothes while residing in the back of beyond. She'd left me a few things I'd never use. But then, a pair of Blundstones that fit perfectly, a cashmere scarf, a few sweatshirts and pants.

I wondered if she wondered about me.

I left my suitcases in the garage. I didn't need anything from my old life.

The man's clothes were still here, too, and I put on one of his flannels. Soft as a lamb's tail. Smelled of juniper and plot twists.

I sat on the sofa for a moment, wondering what to do with myself. I was dying to check social media to see if any of my former friends were discussing me or looking for me. But I hadn't signed up for internet service. Or cable. The flip phone I had was a burner for emergencies, and I'd already lost the charger. I did have a landline installed, also for emergencies. But when I thought about it, it seemed dumb.

Why would I want to be rescued from an emergency?

With none of the old reliable distractions, I decided to treat myself to more wine, a quick smoke on the deck overlooking the wildest and most terrifying country I'd ever seen. I didn't trust the trees. Anything could be hiding back there.

Lesson learned: I wanted to die, but I didn't want to be scared or in any pain. This was helpful information for getting on with the next phase in my plan: Shedding My Mortal Coil.

I was less than twenty-four hours in, but the plan was coming together as if the devil himself had arranged it. I had a tingly little buzz, a jolt of energy from the cigarette, and plenty of poisonous beverages. I'd be dead in no time at this rate. A body my size surely wouldn't sustain week after toxic week of perpetual drunkenness and smoking.

I hoped someone somewhere would say, upon learning of my death, "At least she died doing what she was good at."

Which is the kind of thing Abby would say. Always a touch more chipper than the rest of us, she'd at least made an effort to save me from myself after my diagnosis.

"It's a kit," she said. I had no idea that this "gift" was a precursor to an ambush by the three of them. Apparently, they'd decided my reaction to this little presentation would determine their next steps.

It was a trap.

"When you're feeling up to it," Abby said, "maybe flip through some of these. Perhaps your cancer is a wake-up call to make a change."

I frowned.

This sounded like work.

"You must admit, Tabitha, that before all this, you were on a collision course. It was either this or something worse. Your behavior has been dangerous and self-destructive."

I looked at the stack of books with titles like *The Sobriety Handbook, Trauma Trauma Trauma, You're Not the Main Character, Adulting the Grown-up Way, What Color Is Your Cheese? Narcissist*

No More, and *A Course in Happiness* (upon completion, you get a T-shirt that reads *Kindness Mafia!*).

"Did you clean out the entire self-help section?" I asked, leafing through the pages.

"I carry these at the store. Big money from the wine moms. It's either this or therapy," she said. "You seriously need to rethink your life. And now that you'll be resting, you have the time to read. Look, there are worksheets in some of these."

"Is this because of what happened last month?"

"Tabitha, that was simply one of many incidents that indicate you are in trouble. On its own—horrifying. Absolute nightmare fuel. But when combined with everything else? It's unsustainable. You can't live like this."

She lowered her voice to a whisper even though we were the only two in the room.

"Tabitha, do you comprehend how fucked up it is to tell a kid whose mom is getting married that her new stepdad has arranged for the orphanage to pick her up at the end of the night?"

"It was a boring wedding until that point," I said.

"Amber was traumatized. She's still having nightmares."

"If it helps, I don't remember doing any of that."

"It most definitely does not help," she said. "Opposite, in fact. You chased her with a pool net through a vineyard in the dark. She's five."

How cute that Abby tried to save me with books brimming with psychobabble. I'd gone so far 'round the bend at that point, even a tag team of Carl Jung, Oprah Winfrey, and Meghan Markle couldn't have reeled me back into normalcy.

I was ready to stick a fork in me.

I didn't read the books before the banishment, but I'd brought them with me. I lit some kindling in the soapstone fireplace and tore pages out of each book, one by one, until I was blackout drunk and the pages were gone.

THE NAPA VALLEY isn't Hollywood, but it holds a similar attraction for a certain kind of person. First, it's one of the most beautiful places on the planet, and the weather is nearly always perfect, save for a couple of punishing weeks in the summertime and the occasional wildfire. Basically, any place grapes grow is going to be a nice place to live. Except maybe Hungary.

Second, there are high-paying, glamorous-looking jobs in the wine industry. Granted, the majority of wine industry jobs are not glamorous and are also low paying. But the folks who work in the offices, in the sales, marketing, and PR departments, executives, owners, growers—there was gold in those hills, and it came in the form of rotten grape juice, bottled and marked up a jillion percent.

Me, Serena, Norah, and Abby were all the same age, and we all landed jobs at the same wine marketing agency: Voltaire. We were exactly the kinds of people who emigrated to wine country: bright, savvy, snobby, obsessed with wine and food, and looking to live the good life forever.

We met in onboarding, where it was only the four of us. They chatted like they knew one another already (which they didn't). I felt intimidated right off the bat, so I did the opposite of what a normal person would do and invited myself right into their conversation. This job, this new hometown—fresh starts for me, and I wasn't about to spend my early twenties friendless. I'd already cut ties with everyone I knew in college. Or, rather, they stopped returning my calls.

"You guys want to come over for cocktails tonight at my place?"

They exchanged glances.

"I live right down the block. Could be fun."

"Sure, I'm in," Norah said.

"I can't stay late," Serena said, like always.

Abby chimed in: "I think that sounds nice. I have so many questions about what we're learning here today. I've got no background in wine."

That night the girls came over. I explained some of the wine terms to Abby that she didn't understand, and otherwise told them completely made-up stories about my past.

"Listen to this," Abby said. "Tabitha told me she has a trust fund."

That part was true, but I also told her I'd originally wanted to be a ballerina but broke my foot playing *Giselle*, which I'd never even seen.

"Juicy," Norah said. "What's your trust fund from?"

"Family business," I said. "Pallets."

"Like those wood stacks used in factories?"

"Unbreakable quality—that's Eggs!" I said with a little point of my finger like I was a retro TV pitchman.

They fell out laughing, and I was so happy, my cheeks flushed. Our family company's slogan was more like "Quality Pallets for Quality Customers," but I'd pitched my version at a family dinner once and it went over like a lead balloon.

"That's fucking hilarious," Norah said. "I love it."

By the end of the night, the arrangements had been made. They would all move in as soon as they could.

Because Serena was leaving at a very late hour, she said to me,

"There are some people in this world that exist solely for the rest of us to laugh at. You're one of those people."

I beamed with pride.

————

Those first few years together were a blast.

Our boss called us the "Dream Team." Serena, he said, could organize the liberation of Kuwait with nothing more than a credit card and an internet connection. Norah had a magnificent palate and could identify the most minuscule flavors and aromas in a wine. And Abby could sell water to a fish. I was the writer (natch) and spent my days drafting florid copy for wineries up and down the Napa Valley. If it's on a back label, website, or tasting room menu, I probably wrote it.

"Brisk, refreshing, and bold in its rejection of oak, our Unclothed chardonnay is the essence of sunny Napa Valley, aged in stainless steel. Luscious aromas and flavors shine bright without being hidden behind the flavor of a barrel."

That's the kind of thing I did, and I was good at it. My only problem is that I have a terrible personality, and no one wanted to keep me around long.

We lived together, too, in a ramshackle Victorian with room after room after room, a backyard fire pit, and an enormous, ugly kitchen that was perfect for whipping up apps for all the parties we threw.

My trust fund had set me up nicely to purchase a few friends, so I offered to pay the totality of the rent for all of us if they moved in with me. I continued to do so after they all left to get on with their lives, and that's where I lived still. Until I went to Fort Dick.

I couldn't let it go, even after they all moved out, even after I'd been fired from several good jobs, and even after everyone stopped dropping by for impromptu soirées.

I'd been stuck. I realized that now.

It was great until I got us all fired from Voltaire for sending to them at their work addresses a dirty photo I'd snapped of a coworker in bed. Whoops. Bossman did not like.

It was OK, they'd said. Voltaire was a kind of farm team for bigger things, so those clever gals used this a springboard to get their lives together. I begged them to stay in the Victorian, offered to take on the utilities, but instead, they scattered about and continued to build their careers. So did I, but with one-hundred percent more firings.

Before that, we'd all walk to work together, spend the whole day doing the lord's work in the Napa Valley, and then drink wine, cook, smoke, and sleep around all weekend.

Those days, when we all lived together, were the happiest in my life.

We'd always be hungover on Sunday mornings, so I made it my personal responsibility to deliver ice-cold Coke, ibuprofen, and water to each of them. We'd pile into my big bed (I had the primary suite, of course) and laugh about our adventures.

Laughing is when I felt the closest to people. I was never sure if I could make them like me, was never clear on what it took to be lovable, and I didn't share vulnerabilities to bond. For me, if I could make you laugh, that meant I was worth something.

I didn't want business success like Abby. Or power-coupling like Serena. And I didn't need to climb the corporate ladder like Norah. I didn't want husbands, kids, pets, or any other thing that could tie me down.

Laughter was the only language I understood.

On her moving day, Serena said to me, gravely: "If you're a lesbian, then be a lesbian, OK? We don't care. We're still your friends."

It was like she'd hit me in the chest with her fist. Lesbian?

I'd dallied, of course. I'd gone to an all-girls boarding school, for heaven's sake. I wasn't offended in the slightest by her comment.

Not in that way.

What troubled me was the profound misunderstanding of what made me click.

I didn't pay for them, pamper them, bring them on trips, and otherwise be at their beck and call because I wanted to hop into bed with any of them. I thought they understood what I really wanted.

I wanted sisters.

I'd grown up lonely. The only shared kid of two narcissists who had multiple kids with multiple partners.

I hadn't gotten a call on my birthday in years.

But I did have a trust fund, so for some reason, they thought that meant I had no feelings.

I didn't respond to Serena, probably cementing in her mind that I was in fact a lesbian overcompensating by screwing every guy in the Bay Area because I couldn't find the words to express the depth of my disappointment in this misunderstanding of my motives.

They all left eventually.

Serena, as I mentioned before, was first to fly the coop. She'd fallen in love with the scion of a family-owned wine company called Frog Leg, known for organic something and farm-to-table whatever. She ran herself ragged for that company and for that man. Worth it, I guess, because he proposed to her by presenting her with a business card that had her first name and his last name on it.

"Isn't it beautiful?" she said, admiring the business card.

I spit out my wine.

"You're joking, right?"

The girls looked at me in horror.

"I'm assuming you said no," I said.

"Why would I do that?" Serena asked. She folded her arms across her chest.

"He offered you employment, not a marriage," I said. "Am I the only one seeing this?"

Serena moved into a guest house on her fiancé's family's estate.

Abby was the second to leave the Victorian. She'd arrived in the Napa Valley from Minot, North Dakota, with one goal: to live in a place where people vacationed. She'd had enough of the frigid winters of the Roughrider State, and Napa filled the bill. She diligently saved her Voltaire salary and commissions (because I'd paid her rent for five years), purchased a small space with an apartment above it downtown, and opened a store filled with candles, stationery, and other pretties. She'd never needed to work in the wine industry, she said, but she could see the benefits of being wine country adjacent. Truth is, she made a fortune.

That left me and Norah, who said she was ready to live alone and that we'd be better friends if she didn't have to deal with my "constant rotation of fuck-buddies who left the toilet seat up and ate all our food."

Fair.

Apparently, saving all that rent helped her out, too. She bought a small cottage on Mount Veeder with everything she'd saved, and took a job at a Swiss-owned winery close to her house that had the most magnificent art gallery.

Through all of this, they stuck with me. Until they didn't. They'd each succeeded in their own way, and I was still pottering around an old Victorian, getting fired from every job I ever took, never having a boyfriend, or moving forward at all.

Why did it take me so long to realize they'd tolerated me only because they felt like they owed me?

They did owe me! I may have been a deranged, self-centered, shitfaced slut, and a capital-letter BAD FRIEND, but every single one of those women had succeeded as a direct result of the help I gave them.

Hadn't they?

I'd never thought of it that way before.

None of that mattered now, though. Did it?

CHAPTER
FIVE

CAPTAIN'S LOG, *Day Two of Exile:*

Awoke at the crack of noon with a skull-splitting headache, no doubt induced by the (*omigod*) four bottles of chardonnay and the full pack of American Spirits. I was on the living room floor.

There was vomit.

Probably mine.

After standing on legs as weak as a plover chick's, I wobbled to the kitchen, where I promptly vomited again into the sink.

Drank water. Peed. Stood in the shower with half a glass of chardonnay in a weak attempt to stave off the mean reds.

In the clarity of the afternoon, I realized there was a lot about Kevin I didn't know. I felt mildly comforted by the fact that I owned it. Ownership gave me a sense of belonging I might not have had if I'd rented. Said a silent prayer of thanks for the previous owners and my small trust fund that allowed me to become the hermit I needed to be.

Despite my throbbing head and grinding guts, I appreciated that the crypto failures had exquisite taste. I marveled over the stone countertops and the glittering appliances. They'd clearly wanted a home that reflected the natural beauty that surrounded them, but they didn't get all kitschy with the "cabin" vibe. Not a single sign telling me that I'm in the "Pantry" or that there's "Coffee" in the home. Nary a cross-stitch sampler, a rocking chair, or any plastic lawn furniture to be found.

The floors were polished concrete, the high ceilings had exposed beams, and the carpet in the bedrooms was hand knotted out of alpaca wool. It felt like walking on a puffy cloud. I wanted to lie down on it and allow its fibers to devour me inch by inch.

Instead, I paced.

From what I could remember, the previous night had been strange. I was officially a book burner, and as a writer, this was a twist I'd never predicted. It was a blur. But I did remember this: I popped out several times to smoke on the redwood deck, which was surrounded by the deepest, darkest blackness I'd ever experienced. Like stepping into a black hole.

I did this for hours. The last time I saw the clock, it was three in the morning.

But something odd—

I was sucking on my lung dart, shivering against the chill, and talking to myself to alleviate the oppressiveness of the absolute silence, when I heard something.

Howling. Or barking. Shrieking? Or howl-bark-shrieking? It was probably coyotes combined with a psychosis-inducing amount of chaptalized plonk, but maybe not?

It was at once piercing, mournful, and otherworldly. Ancient and wild.

I could still feel it in my bones.

I shivered at the memory and threw up on my feet.

CHAPTER
SIX

"YOU DON'T HAVE A DRINKING PROBLEM," Norah said at brunch after a night of debauchery. "You drink as much as the rest of us. You, Tabitha, have a big-mouth problem. And frankly, it's getting annoying. No one can trust you. You spill everyone's secrets."

"I can't have you calling me at sunrise every morning after a party and asking me if you did anything embarrassing," Abby chimed in. "From now on, assume the answer is always yes. Yes. You did something embarrassing."

"Oh, god," I said, head in hands, waiting for the mimosa to kick in, hair of the dog. "What was it this time?"

"When I found you, you were reading Mel Staples the riot act for cheating on his wife and always being sloppy drunk."

"It was a real pot-kettle-black moment, in my opinion," said Abby, taking a bite of her beet salad. "Pretty funny."

I couldn't even respond.

"You know he has a speech impediment, right?" Norah said. "That's why he slurs. And then, when you said everyone knew he was cheating, it was like, where'd you get that info? You out there, slandering people for no reason?"

"He's my boss," I said. "And I see his expense reports."

"I'd wager he *was* your boss," Norah said. "How many jobs is this now? Three?"

"Four," I said. "How can I face him Monday?"

"Like you do everything," Serena said. "You don't. I'll bet you $500 you won't go in on Monday to own up to what you've done."

"You're on," I said. "My humiliation knows no bounds. And I might need the five hundo."

Turns out I did. Mel wasn't in when I arrived at the office on Monday, but my things were neatly packed and waiting for me at reception.

Serena didn't respond to my Venmo request.

Funny thing was, I was the one sleeping with Mel.

CHAPTER
SEVEN

WHAT I WOULDN'T HAVE DONE for a burrito. Or a burger. I can't remember the last time I had to prepare food for myself when I was this hungover. Whole new world and all that. I cracked open a Coke, popped my nachos in the microwave, and ate it all standing up. Followed by four Advil and a quick smoke on the deck, and I'd be right as rain and ready to die feeling great.

As I lit my ciggie, I noticed a hulking, spooky thing in my backyard. I felt as if I'd seen it last night, but I didn't fully register it in my inebriated state. It was a concrete cylinder, about fifteen feet high and nearly ten feet across. I walked over to it and knocked on it a few times, accomplishing nothing more than scraping my knuckles.

Nothing knocked back.

Not yet anyway.

And that smell! The rotting-redwood duff-and-decaying-road-kill smell. It reminded me of the time I left a piece of leftover lunch chicken in my desk drawer, and the office manager thought it was a dead rat in the walls.

Was it coming from this tank?

I called stupid Annie.

"Hey, it's Tabitha," I said. "Hate to bug. But what's this Soviet-era missile silo in my yard?"

"I'm sorry, what's in your yard?"

"A proper description would be a concrete tank of unknown origin."

"Of course," Annie said, her voice slightly cheerier than before. "That's your water."

"Come again?"

"Your water tank. That's the water that gives your house, you know, water."

"For, like, firefighting?"

"Yes, that too. But your showers and everything. You have a well that goes down to the bedrock and you pull your water from there. A red gauge on the side tells you your levels."

"So, I will literally use this to put out a raging mountain fire on my own, and I also have to monitor it so that I don't run out."

"Correct," she said "You're too far up the mountain to have access to city water. You have a well. A lot of people do. This information was in the disclosures you signed."

"I'm not mad about it, Annie. I'm curious."

"Of course," she said, smoothing the edges in her tone. "I can send someone out to show you how it operates."

One hour later, I was standing on top of my water tank with Dick from Fort Dick General Store, wishing I'd taken a few more Advil. He showed me how to test the water for hardness and how to attach the fire-ready hose in case a raging inferno was racing down the hill toward me.

"Douse the whole house," he said. "It's already fire hardened with the right siding, sprinklers on the metal roof, and all that. You know a fire's coming, best thing is to get out. The house may or may not be OK, but better not to stick around to see it."

"You're saying this like it's definitely going to happen."

"That's about all there is to know," he said. "Water goes in from below. You use it. End of story."

He started to climb down.

"Always a pleasure, Dick," I said. "Quick question. Do you notice a weird smell? I think there might be kids up here smoking weed in the woods. Or skunks, maybe? Not that I mind either, but I do want to know what I'm dealing with. Skunk? Human? Underground methane plume?"

"Something like that," he said. "You'll get used to it."

"But what if teenagers lighting joints sets my mountain on fire? What then, Dick? Who will save me, Dick? Is it you? Oh, woe is me."

Either Dick is hard of hearing, or he's got ninja-level ignoring skills.

I was still standing on the top of the water tank when Dick got into his banged-up Toyota Tundra and drove down the hill.

He was in a hurry.

I'D NEVER FELT MORE love in my life than when Norah, Abby, and Serena came with me to a high-end salon to get manis, pedis, and massages—and to get my head shaved before starting chemotherapy.

"All this beautiful hair," Abby said. "You're so brave. You sure you want to do this? No second thoughts?"

As my blonde tresses fell gently to the floor, there wasn't a dry eye to be found at Salon Cuvée. Even my stylist was crying. The receptionist. A few randos wandering around. Everyone said something to me about staying strong and being a warrior. For once, I wasn't the friend apologizing for making out with someone's brother or for falling into the pool at the baby shower. I was the friend these lovely women rallied around. They were rooting for me to get better, and I was mad about all of them.

I was conveniently funemployed when this whole escapade began, having been terminated in a round of layoffs that affected a few people at the company who all seemed to have something in common: no one liked us. I knew the layoff was an excuse to clear the decks when my copywriting position was filled within three weeks. Confirmed when my former boss asked me for coffee to "see how I was doing" and then told me that "sometimes, like dating, certain personalities aren't a match for corporate culture."

"No one liked me," I said. "I get it."

"That puts a fine point on it, but basically, yes."

Then, "I'm actually trying to help you."

"Help me what? Get my job back?"

She broke into laughter. "Oh, heavens, no. That ship has sailed. The new gal is amazing."

My layoff didn't engender too much sympathy among the gal pals. My track record with that was bleak. But a cancer diagnosis? They rallied like an underdog football club.

Our wine gatherings took place at my house because I was so weak and whatever. They came around with bags filled with groceries, vitamins, herbal supplements, movies, magazines—everything a convalescing lady of leisure could want. Drove me to appointments. Texted all day and brought me warm, fuzzy things to wear. Told hilarious stories about work and shared all the juicy gossip. They took time away from the things that truly mattered to them to build me up, keep me healthy, and fight cancer. They were angels who'd seen past my infinite flaws and to the human underneath who wanted only one thing: to live.

I didn't deserve them.

No, seriously. I did not.

My friends were getting married, starting businesses, becoming goddesses of industry. All that time, I was working as little as possible and partying my face off. We were all the exact same age—thirty-three—but they were moving gracefully through the normal development stages while I was stuck in adolescence.

Living here, in this dark forest, was my chance to improve, earn their trust.

But I wasn't going to improve, make good, get better, or evolve out of sheer spite.

I didn't want to do any of the work. Nothing inspired me.

I'll show myself out, thanks.

I took a deep sip of wine and stepped outside onto the patio. The sun was setting, and the moon was rising. I let rip a howl for the ages, my mournful cry for the past I could never recover. Distant, recent, it didn't matter. I howled and shook and stomped my feet. I gnashed my teeth and rolled around on the deck. *Awooooo. Awoooo.*

I felt frenzied, but not same the frenzy I felt when I was partying or stealing attention or needing to be the main character. It was a private frenzy that allowed me to feel something new. My life force. My anger. My need. And I howled on and on and on.

Something howled back.

I was hearing things, right?

I howled again, perfect movie-style werewolf howl, very dramatic.

Nothing.

Oh, well, I thought. Animals don't want to talk to a drunk dying lady. They have their own lives to live.

My glass was nearly empty. "Can't have that," I said, quietly patting myself on the back for being so well stocked.

I heard it again.

A howl, imitating mine.

I howled back, my hand on the doorknob.

This is fun, I thought. I believed I'd made a coyote friend and was bracing myself for all kinds of trickster pranks out here in the woods.

When it howled again, it was deeper, richer. Not an imitation.

Not even a howl.

A low rumble at a pitch that was less heard than felt passed through me, vibrating my organs. The ground rattled under my feet.

And then a shrieking scream echoed in my ears so loudly I covered them.

My feet still unsteady from the tectonic shift under them, I stepped inside the house, pulled the door closed, and locked it as swiftly as I could.

I wondered if I'd remember this in the morning.

I hoped I wouldn't.

CHAPTER
NINE

THE BOREDOM WAS REAL.

The chatter in my mind was a scurry of chipmunks, running one self-destructive idea after another like a dress rehearsal.

"*Call them. Call them. Call them,*" my brain—a naughty devil —urged.

Either I couldn't sit still or I could *only* sit still. Who knew that ditching your cell phone and the internet and cutting yourself off from everyone you ever knew would result in infinite free time?

I'd been indoors for more than a week now, save for smoking outside and obsessively checking the water tank levels.

I was alone with my memories, and my memories were being bullies.

I was essentially unlovable. Not in the oh-woe-is-me way, but something fundamental about me was off. I didn't get it. I didn't understand how to be in the world. I winged it with a mix of try-hard, overcompensation, dishonesty, and joking.

And all I had now was a wine-shaped hole that I'd done a very good job of filling on that particular day.

I could barely walk, much less go for a hike in the woods. Wasn't that the point, though? To die here? It seemed a waste to not spend time in my private aerie, but there was also no need to drag this out if this is how I was going to feel every day.

What, exactly, was there to live for?

I had nothing to look forward to.

Today's the day, I decided. I slogged back half a bottle of wine followed by four or five shots of vodka. I grabbed a handle of vodka, stuffed a pack of smokes into my pocket, and took to the woods.

What better way to die than hammered and surrounded by ferns?

I thought I'd wait until my health woes were irreversible, my skin jaundiced the sickly yellow of old paper, and my desperate liver and singed lungs crying uncle. I'd walk out into the unforgiving wilderness, fall asleep, and never come back.

Come on in, little critters, my decomposing corpse would say. Lay your eggs in my ears. Plant your fungal spores in my nasal cavities. Build bacterial colonies as complex as our universe. And nibble my organs from the inside out. I'm useful. And I'm all yours.

Walking, according to the experts, was the universal cure-all. If I could implement about a half hour of walking per day into my routine, I'd remove negative thoughts, eat healthier, have a positive attitude, be more productive.

Or get murdered on a trail.

It's what we call a win-win for someone in my circumstance.

I pulled up my big-girl panties, laced up my sassy sneaks, and strode out to die.

The first few hundred yards were shaky. Walking through mostly untouched woods wasn't at all like walking the mall.

I'd never been alone in the woods. Never had to contend with the silence that wraps around you like a sopping wet blanket. Nothing but the sound of trees creaking to keep me company. Nothing but my own dark thoughts to urge me on.

I stumbled onward, not sure what I was looking for—only that I needed a place to sit comfortably. The handle of vodka was getting heavy. Small movements from the corners of my eyes—birds, probably—startled me.

I was fully shit-faced; the trail undulated before me. Roots popped up out of nowhere, tripping me, causing me to cradle the huge bottle of vodka like a baby to prevent it from breaking and ruining my plan.

My knees were muddy. My hands were scraped.

I vomited more than once and washed out my guts with more and more vodka.

It burned. My throat was ablaze.

I could sense the event horizon. Blackout was imminent.

Perfect.

For a brief, incandescent moment, I changed my mind.

I could turn around right now and blunder back to Kevin. I could make a proper dinner in my Nancy Meyers kitchen. I'd wear a caftan and roast a chicken. Whip up a salad. Perhaps take up barefoot trail running, like that tall guy in Mexico or Peter Sarsgaard or whoever it was. I laughed out loud at that. I don't think I'd ever run more than fifteen steps in my life, and that was only because I was trying to get to the bar before last call.

No, a voice deep inside my mind said clearly. *That life's not for you.*

Resigned and ready, I tromped away from anything that could be considered a trail and crouched down behind a boulder. I lit a cigarette. Drank some more, even though the alcohol was strafing my guts.

The tears flowed; my eyes swelled. I couldn't stop. I was utterly overwhelmed with the beauty of this place, of my place in it, and all my failures.

I took a few more deep breaths, apologized silently to my dusty lungs and my poisoned heart.

And that's when I saw it.

An object caught a sunbeam and sparkled.

"Ooh, shiny," I slurred.

I felt a small pang in my chest. That's what the girls and I used to say when any of us showed up with new jewelry.

That's when I noticed the smell. Sickly sweet. Garlicky. It was equally pungent as the smell I'd noticed around the house, but different. Meatier. Rottier. Fleshier. Now with more gag-inducing chemicals.

I moved closer.

The shiny object was a watch.

The watch was attached to a wrist.

The wrist was missing its skin.

It was also missing the elbow, shoulder, and the rest of the body.

I gasped.

I was surrounded by body parts and the remains of what appeared to be two tracksuits, torn to ribbons.

And flies. Everywhere flies.

Three hands, a foot still snug in a Merrell trail boot. A length of tangled strawberry blonde hair that had cascaded out of a copse of blackberries. Some bones picked clean, wet, and shiny from dew.

An empty eye socket, bone peeking through, surrounded by small, brown mushrooms. Maggots writhing in a blue-green male torso a few feet away.

The smell threatened to overwhelm me. Waves of nausea, painful like a stab, pounded my abdomen.

I thought maybe two bodies altogether, but possibly more. Parts were scattered about. A gooey toenail atop a fern. A finger covered in mold.

Carnage.

This is what I craved for myself.

Wasn't it?

This is exactly how they'd find me.

If they found me.

For the first time on my walk (in my life?), I had no words. My mind was a perfect blank.

And for the first time in my life, I ran home.

CHAPTER
TEN

"WHAT IN THE I'm-calling-my-lawyer fuckery is this, Annie?" I slurred into the phone at the stupid realtor I'd never met. "Aren't you legally required to disclose this information?"

Naturally, after I bolted down the mountain like a goat racing an avalanche (falling more than once and skinning my delicate knees repeatedly), I called 911. Within two hours, the area was crawling with teams of people with radios, jackets, and latex gloves. Overeager Malinois tugged at leashes, their handlers shouting brisk commands.

I wanted nothing to do with any of it. Poured myself a drink. Offered my observations to some officer, but what else was there for me to do? According to the uniforms, this was probably the crypto couple. Apparently, they'd been missing for a while.

I couldn't get the images out of my mind or the rage out of my chest. I called Annie to unleash hell.

"You didn't tell me the previous owners were missing! What the fuckety fuck? I went forest bathing and tripped over two rotting bodies."

I said the forest-bathing part as a humblebrag, like I'm definitely a Zen guru and not a nearly blacked-out suicidal drunk.

"Tabitha," she said in that irritating tone people use when

they're trying to calm you down. "When you called and said you saw the house online and that nothing else mattered but the Meyer lemon kitchen, I believed you."

"Nancy Meyers," I corrected. "How can you call yourself a realtor and not be familiar with the decorative stylings of Nancy Meyers? *The Holiday*? Come on."

"You paid with cash," she continued. "We closed in ten days with no inspections. You didn't ask what happened to the previous owners. The only thing you cared about was getting their furniture. Which you did. And a lot of other things."

"Is that something buyers usually ask? If the previous owners are putrefying in a maggot-infested heap somewhere in the back forty? I didn't think I'd need to inquire about that kind of thing, Annie."

"Realtors are required to disclose when there has been a death in the home."

"Annie, I need you to be honest with me. Do I need to be afraid for my life?"

This might all go much easier than I thought. Some homicidal maniac breaks in, and murdering me to death might engender sympathy in some people in my life who may not have many reasons to feel lovingly toward me.

I decided to leave all the doors unlocked. Just in case.

"What do you mean?" she asked.

"Is there someone up here, on this quiet mountain, behind a tiny town bustling with secrets, murdering people who live in this house?"

She remained silent.

I thought about my funeral and how the girls would say something along the lines of I was "misunderstood" and "vibrant" and "taken too soon."

Then I remembered when my eleventh-grade teacher asked if any of us had had daydreams about what people would say at our funerals.

Every girl in the class raised her hand.

"Grow up," she said, and she returned to the lesson.

If I knew anything about Serena, Norah, and Abby, they would hear the news, be sad for about eight minutes, and then wonder where all my money went.

That's not a dig on them. That's what they should do.

"Annie, I'm afraid. Should I be afraid right now? That someone will harm me?"

This was all for show. You never know when you might need to file a lawsuit.

"There's no person in Fort Dick that will hurt you, Tabitha."

I caught the phrasing, and I became enraged.

"What is it then? Mountain lion? Bear? What the fuck? And if you say bigfoot, I swear I am going to come down there and kick over your trash can."

She cleared her throat.

I sat down on the floor to collect myself and realized I wasn't asking the right questions.

"What kind of scheme are you running here, Annie?"

"What do you mean?" she asked.

"Did you have authorization to sell this house to me?"

Silence.

I was borderline joking, trying to shake her out of her stonewalling.

Her reaction spooked me.

"Annie. Did you? Have permission to sell me this house?" I started to sweat. I'd spent most of what I had left on this house. Had I been scammed?

"Are you even a realtor?"

Of course she wasn't. Any modern real estate agent worth the price of a lockbox would know exactly what a Nancy Meyers kitchen is.

I heard a sound like someone tapping a stack of papers together. A drawer closing.

"The house is yours, free and clear," she said, finally. "Your name is on the title, which is legally filed with Del Norte County."

"Annie," I said, as my intestines tied themselves into a knot. "Did you, or did you not, have authorization to sell me this house?"

"The previous owners were child-free. Their living parents are in care homes overseas. There's no one to challenge your right to the house."

"Annie! Answer me."

"I'm going to say this one time, and one time only," she said, her voice quavering. "You own the house. There aren't any more questions you need to ask. Your questions won't hurt anyone but you. Do you understand me?"

"Annie, I—"

The line went dead.

CHAPTER ELEVEN

THE FLASHING LIGHTS and other hubbub from official people continued late into the night.

I hated myself. This whole situation was so Tabitha. Once again, I'd failed to consider all the variables.

This had always been too good to be true.

Of course the owners had gone missing, presumed dead, and an unscrupulous person had taken advantage of the situation. Did this mean that Annie took all my cash? It wasn't even a commission; she got all of it! I hoped it had been worth it. From where I was sitting, it seemed like she'd led me to slaughter.

Good for her, I guess. There are winners and there are losers in this world, and I now knew which column I was in.

Had always been, despite my shiny wrapping.

As the hours ticked by and my situation became clear, I ran through some scenarios in my head.

I could leave. Pack my bags tonight and head out in the morning.

Unfortunately, I had nowhere to go and very little money left. I could try begging one of the girls to take me in for a while.

I couldn't tolerate the thought of having that conversation.

That was a dead end. No going back there.

Parents were out. They'd lost interest in parenting years ago, and both were living with their third or fourth spouses wherever they were now. Both of them would think I was asking for money from the prodigious Eggs family pallets fortune.

Also a dead end.

And that was it. I didn't even have a cell phone to flip through to see if there was anyone, anywhere who could assist me.

What would I tell them anyway? This story was ludicrous.

After I unscrewed the cap on my wine, though, it dawned on me.

This was exactly where I was called to be.

Why was I so afraid of death at the hands of a mysterious lurker, when only a few hours before I'd wandered out there, totally ready to die?

Being murdered could take care of my problems with zero effort.

Kinda scary, sure. But there are two kinds of women in the world: the kind who are afraid of being murdered for walking around and the kind that get murdered for walking around.

However, I'm a white woman of privilege, and therefore I steadfastly believe that the universe rearranges itself to my benefit. Clearly, I'd been put in this situation as a test.

If I survived what was out there, I could sell Kevin by owner, recoup my money, and then go back into the world fresh and shiny as a new penny.

If I didn't survive—well, then I failed the test.

Emboldened by this deal with my personal devil, I stepped outside into the cold, dark night and released another confident howl.

The sound echoed through the forest like an alarm, and only a few moments—or was it hours?—passed before whatever was out there howled back.

"Come and get me!" I shouted to the night. "I have nothing to live for! *Awooooooooo!*"

I laughed and laughed, waiting for a simple response from the universe.

I turned to go inside, when I felt hot breath on the top of my head.

"Ogh," it grunted, blasting me with the scent of dental distress.

The universe had answered.

Tall as a bear. Warmth emanated from its body.

For a half second, I leaned back, hoping whatever it was would end me now. Grab my chin like in the movies and give one hard twist. I'd crumple to the ground.

Instead, it stepped away.

My senses recovered.

I stepped through, slammed the door, turned off the lights. I looked outside.

Whatever it was was gone.

I collapsed onto the floor. Terror overtook me, and I couldn't breathe.

Maybe I wasn't as ready as I thought.

CHAPTER
TWELVE

THE MORNING after I found the two desiccating, dismembered corpses of the exceedingly tasteful people who formerly lived in my house was a shit show.

The story had made the eleven o'clock news, and my fortress of solitude had been invaded by countless flannel-clad, red-hatted men, most of them carrying guns.

There was also a small gathering of crunchy-looking folk holding signs that read *"They Were Here First," "Peace with Our First Inhabitants,"* and *"Keep Your Small Hands off Our Bigfoot."*

I saw Dick and waved him over. "What's going on here, Dick?"

"I came to check it out myself. How're you doing?"

He seemed concerned, and I felt bad for mocking him in my mind. I had to remind myself again that I wasn't the main character in this story. I was a lady with a house on a mountain where two people were mangled, asking a question of another not-main character. I could let my guard down, and I did.

"It's scary," I said, like a normal person who didn't believe in a tiny bit of her brain that being attacked by a serial murderer would make this last bit much easier. "Did you know when you met me that the owners had gone missing?"

He shook his head. "No, I did not. I certainly would've had an opinion about that. That Annie keeps her cards close to her vest."

"You know her," I said. A statement. Of course he knows her. There are fewer than five hundred full-time residents here.

"Not really," he said, "She's here and there."

I decided not to press the issue of the legality of the home sale. What Annie had told me about questions was more of a threat than I was willing to poke at, so I asked instead what all these people were doing running around in the woods when they should be at home in bed with a hangover—which is where I'd like to be.

"They've gone squatchin'," he said.

"Who's done what now?" I asked.

"Squatchin'. Bigfoot hunting."

"Is this like a festival or something? Bigfest? Run around the redwoods and look for cryptids? Like a snipe hunt?"

"It's no festival," he said. "And no joke. Those cryptos—sorry, their names were Krista and Ben, may they rest in peace—may have been mauled on that trail. And some folks out here think that means a bigfoot did it."

"You're not serious," I said. "They aren't serious, right? It's ridiculous."

"Not to them it's not. Those hunters mean business. So do the protesters. They want our local population to be left alone. It's one of the last remaining colonies."

"You mean to tell me that all the bigfoot shops and statues and tours—you believe all that? It's not simply a fun joke that you all play along with?"

"It's not fun. And it's no joke," he said.

"You think that *Harry and the Hendersons* are up here tearing people limb from limb?"

I'd never noticed before how blue his eyes were as he stared at me like he was boring a hole through my skull.

"We don't talk about that with the visitors," he said. "But you live here now. In that house. The one we told them not to build here. Annie should be ashamed of herself, not telling you. But you're in the middle of their home. And they were here first."

"You're telling me I overpaid for a house in the middle of Chewbacca's dining room?"

Dick looked offended.

"Chewbacca is a Wookiee. Listen, I'm telling you to be careful. It's possible those two were set upon by a big cat. Maybe a bear."

"Dick, be honest," I said. "Do you believe that bigfoot did this?" I asked, preparing to roll my eyes hard enough to see my brain stem.

Old habit. I hadn't processed my experience from last night, and now was not the time. I simply would not believe that I was breathed on by bigfoot. I was a late-stage alcoholic. Probably a hallucination.

Dick's attitude shifted in a way I could sense. He seemed calm, reverent, like he was relaying a message he'd received from an alien. "I know they're peaceful," he said. "They'd have to be intensely provoked to attack a human or utterly starving. But having said that, if they were cornered, they could end your life with one swipe. That's it. Lights out."

"Lights out from a made-up thing?" I asked. "Do I have to worry about drop bears? Chupacabra? Mothman?"

"If you don't believe, that's on you," he said, turning to leave. "I don't have the energy to argue."

I recognized this as a learning moment and decided to back-track. I had offended Dick—I knew it—and one of the things good people did was apologize. I didn't want to believe in all this crap, but that's no reason to belittle someone else.

"Hey, wait," I said. "I'm sorry." The words felt odd in my mouth, like an off-brand candy. Sweet, but kind of off. I'd made a clever quip that showed off my knowledge of cryptids, and I'd never felt the need to apologize for that kind of comment before. But here we were. "I realize that I'm new here and have much to learn about the area. Tell me, Dick. Do you think I'm safe?"

"Depends," he said. "Do you want to be out here alone, knowing you're in their yard?"

"Do you think that whoever did that to the cryptos—"

"Krista and Ben," he said.

"Right. Do you think this targeted them specifically? Or anyone in the house? Could it possibly be human? Maybe they were involved in something shady?"

"I couldn't speculate," he said. "But it's not a chance I'd take. Human or animal."

I shivered at his tone. He wasn't kidding. At all.

"No sleepover for you then," I said, wrapping my arms around myself. "But I don't have much choice. I'll let you know if I see one."

"No, you won't," Dick said. "It'll be the last thing you ever see."

THE SQUATCHIN' didn't die down for a few weeks. The die-hard sasquatch hunters tromped through my property at every hour of the day and night, asking directions, looking for bathrooms, hoping for a meal. The protesters kept things more polite. They brought their own sandwiches like civilized people. The random tourists who happened to be in town during a bigfoot flare-up looked lost and confused.

I played along a little.

"Oh, you just missed 'em," I told a wide-eyed couple in a rented Ford Focus. "A mama and twins. Walked right through here, waved, and then disappeared."

"Are twins common?" The female asked, as if this was a real conversation.

"It depends," I said, rubbing my chin like I was the forest docent. "With climate change, we've started to see more twins and triplets. Not sure if it's a good thing or not." I pounded on the roof of their car, dismissing them. "You folks take care now, and remember to recycle. Anything to help our squatch brothers and sisters, amirite?"

I wished I had internet so I could do a little research. Instead, I let my imagination take the wheel. Were they out there right now?

A family—a colony!—of tall, fuzzy ape-guys who want to be left alone but who react violently when they aren't? How did they hide? What did they do all day? Did they have a language?

Did I believe in bigfoot now? Because a rando townie said they're out there?

That didn't explain the throngs of people swarming my mountain, though. As the excitement continued around me, I was more afraid of the hunters than I was the sasquatch. I stayed inside all day and drank. I wasn't here to track down myths, I reminded myself.

I wouldn't admit this if you'd asked me at that point, but I was bummed that I'd burned my self-help books.

What could they have said? I already knew I was the poster child for main-character syndrome. What if I practiced being a side character for a while? What would that look like?

I tried it on like an ill-fitting coat.

"Hello, what is your name?" I asked the mirror. I realized I was still centering myself in the conversation because it was me asking me. I moved away from the mirror and walked through Kevin, reciting what I thought might be good questions to ask people that (1) would get them to open up about themselves, (2) would teach me how they like to be spoken to, and (3) wouldn't imply that I wanted anything other than to get to know them.

"Where are you from?" I asked the kitchen counter. "What's it like there?"

"How did you end up in your current job?" I inquired of the stove. "What do you do all day?"

"You're going on a trip to Rome?" I asked the sink. "I can't wait to hear what it's like."

I waited for the other shoe to drop. Surely, now that I was having some fun, it would end.

I'd felt like a new woman on my silly walk the other day. Until I stumbled over two dead bodies.

I wasn't allowed to feel good.

The drinking, the partying, the joking around, the refusal to take my life seriously—all of that was about feeling good.

Laughter *was* my love language. I'd do anything to make people laugh. At me.

I'd humiliate myself before *you* could. Laugh at my messiness, my shame, my stupidity. I was in on the joke.

Wasn't I?

It never worked. Not for long, anyway.

And now, I was thoroughly alone.

The enormity and permanence of my losses were wrecking balls to my sternum.

It was time for an ugly cry. The kind of cry that requires a decision at the end. A revelation. The villain has a change of heart, and her heart grows three sizes.

It came on fast, like a monster reached up, gripped my guts, and pulled me toward the floor, where I heaved and thrashed and gulped for air for what felt like hours. I wore myself out.

The unmistakable pop of gunfire woke me up.

I hoisted myself off the floor, took a sec to get my bearings, and crawled to the back window.

Beflanneled hunters caromed down the mountain, waving their guns in a way that led me to believe they weren't applying best safety practices. Aside from the random, spine-tingling cracks that echoed through the forest, the hunters were silent. Panicked. Hustling. But silent.

I stayed low. There was gunfire after all, and with my luck, I'd get hit and live through it. I watched until I saw the last man, alone, wandering as though he was in shock. He slowly lumbered back and forth, dazed as a hatchling, toward my back patio (fieldstone, with a hand-built pizza oven—it was unbelievably nice), where he collapsed, possibly from the shock of losing his left arm.

"Oh. Oh, my. Shit," I said, getting up from the floor. I took the smallest of microseconds to shift my attention—from the blood pool that would surely leave a stain—to the fact that there was a human being who needed help.

My help.

For the second time in a month, for the second time in my life, I dialed 911.

As they were on their way, I went outside to sit with the patient.

"What's your name?" I asked.

He grunted something that sounded like "Morpheumgrun," and a clot of blood slipped out of his mouth and plopped onto the patio. It jiggled slightly.

"What happened to you?" I asked.

I silently hoped he'd say something like, "I fell into a ravine," or "Momma bear" or "It's only a flesh wound."

He became completely still for a few moments until he started to seize, which scared me more than anything I'd ever seen in my entire life. His eyes rolled back, and his body clenched into an impossible position. I heard his joints crack.

Overcome by something I would later realize was compassion, I put my hands on his remaining arm, hoping to calm him.

It worked.

He stopped convulsing and stared into space.

"Morpheumgrun?" I asked.

He didn't move. I watched for anything that might be breath.

And as I leaned in to listen for a heartbeat, he jolted one last time, looked me dead in the eyes and said,

"You'd better run, little boy."

I DIDN'T RUN. Not then.

I heard later that Morpheumgrun, whose given name was Murphy Grundladge, went to his ease in the ambulance ride to Sutter Coast Hospital.

I stayed.

The mountain cleared of people. No one, not even the gun-toting yahoos, wanted to tangle with what lived in my backyard.

I remained on high alert. I'd received no news about the investigation into Krista and Ben's deaths, partially because I wasn't looking for any, partially because that topic seemed to set the few people I spoke with on edge. Mostly Dick, if I'm honest. He became noticeably flustered if I mentioned it while stocking up on general store goods.

I didn't want to talk about sasquatch. Or dead homeowners. Or Morpheumgrun's dying from—something. Or the fact that I might not legally own my home.

As the weeks passed, I settled into a life of deep quiet, punctuated by intense emotional outbursts.

When I blew through four cases of wine in three weeks—and I didn't want to drive down the mountain—I didn't refill my selection. Alcohol free for the first time in more than a decade, I sweat through my sheets for six straight nights, practically hallucinated, and otherwise experienced a dangerous detox that no doubt could have and probably should have killed me.

Quitting drinking is no joke, kiddos. And after wringing buckets of sweat out of the Frette sheets for days, I still couldn't say I was ready to give it up forever.

I felt better and was sleeping better than I ever had in my life. I hadn't taken up walking again because of the—*ahem*—dead bodies littering the trails. But with nothing but hours to fill, I did yoga, cleaned, and masturbated like it was my job.

I was still smoking, though.

Progress, not perfection, amirite?

Anyhoo, the final thing that needed tackling was my mother-fucking water tank.

Remember her? The ten-foot-high concrete cylinder that holds water pumped straight out of the ground like some Laura Ingalls shit? Situated outside my bedroom, the water tank was the only blemish on this otherwise flawless piece of property.

No one is questioning the importance of water, but this behemoth begged the question: Why so ugly?

I'd never get the answer to that, but I imagined the crypto duo had plans to cover the outside with a facade of hand-foraged gnome poop or something. But that wasn't my main problem. My issue with the water tank was the noise it made as it filled up.

Imagine it: You're drifting off to sleep, sober as a newborn. You're going through all the things you're looking forward to doing the next day or fantasizing about a guy you like, when out of nowhere, the GIANT WATER TANK OUTSIDE YOUR WINDOW STARTS GLUGGING.

And then continues to glug away in roughly thirty-second increments every forty-five minutes.

It wasn't just glugging, either. An ear-splitting grinding sound happened before and after the glug.

I hadn't noticed it when I was passing out drunk every night.

The sound jolted me out of sleep every time, and the adrenaline from being startled kept me awake for hours.

I thought about what was out there and wondered whether it was also thinking about me.

Surely, this tank didn't need to be *gloggluggloogjng* all the livelong day and night to supply tiny me with enough water to live.

I did what any sane person would do.

I turned off the well pump.

Temporarily, of course. I'd flip the switch back on when the water got low.

I can almost hear your thoughts. Why on earth is this weirdo sharing these excruciatingly dull details about home care and maintenance? If you wanted this kind of information, you'd have watched a home improvement show. Surely, you'd rather hear the story about how I shit my Lululemons trying to squirm myself into crow pose while I was in spontaneous alcohol detox or a detailed exploration into the final blow of my ten-year friendships, but that's something I'll have to address later if I stumble into a good segue.

The water tank is the upturned nail on the bottom step. It's what happens when Gwyneth makes it onto the train—or doesn't. It's this story's choice between black or red. Chekhov's gun.

And now that you've seen it, you're not going to believe what happened in there.

"YOU'RE BEING A SEX PEST," Serena commented to me at one of the parties at her fiancé's swanky vineyard cottage. "Stop it or I'll send you home. Again."

"You're going to send me home?" I slurred. "There are, like, six people snorting coke in your bathroom right now."

"But they aren't dry humping everyone in the house," she spat. "Stay off people. You look ridiculous. Hunter's complaining."

She had a valid point. I was very loose, sexually speaking, and I aimed to bring someone, anyone home with me that night. Unfortunately, I'd pregamed pretty hard and showed up to her place single and ready to tingle.

Numerous possibilities were in attendance, including cute Hunter (who for some reason was being a puss), and I was making it no secret what my endgame was.

My flirting game was intense. I'd sit in laps and lick ears. I used sushi rolls as "eyes" and walked around the room saying, "Can sushi me?" I straight-up asked a handsome fella I'd never met before if he wanted to go to my place.

Seems like he did, because before I knew it, he was throwing me all around my bedroom like I was a ragdoll. I had no idea how we'd even gotten there, but the next morning he was gone, my car keys were on the kitchen counter, and there were fifteen messages and thirty-two texts on my phone.

The girls were big mad, and they insisted I meet them for lunch. This was a pattern. I'd have too much fun, they'd get annoyed, I'd buy them all lunch and take them shopping, and all would be forgiven.

This particular hangover was a force of nature.

They said to meet them at this Mexican place in Yountville that had Chihuahua-sized burritos, and I was totally down for that.

I had no idea I was walking into a firestorm.

They were waiting for me when I arrived., each one looking neat, tidy, and not the least bit affected by the events of the party the night before. They sat with their hands primly folded in front of them on the table.

I sat down.

"So," I began. "What's new?"

Norah began. "How many people have you fucked this year, Tabitha?"

"Could I get a Coke before the intervention?" I asked, while waving over a server I'd spent a weekend with a few months prior. Ted, I think.

Serena rolled her eyes. "How was it with Enzo last night?"

"Was that his name?"

He was cute.

Serena slammed her hands on the table. "Tabitha, for fuck's sake. Are you going to jump into bed with every single man in the Napa Valley? I invited Enzo to meet Abby."

"You should've told me," I said. I looked around for my soda. Where was Ted? And then: "Oh, wow. I see that now. He'd be great for you, Abby."

But we all knew that wouldn't have changed anything. I'd slept with nearly every guy the girls were interested in.

"I did tell. Several times." Serena looked like she might launch across the table.

My Coke arrived, I sucked it down without coming up for air, and motioned to Ted to get me a refill, stat.

Abby placed a hand on Serena's wrist. "Tabitha, we've been talking."

Oh, god. My stomach churned.

She continued: "We all need to step back from our relationship. We can't babysit you anymore. You're thirty-three. And you act like you're perpetually on spring break."

"I am," I said. My mouth was filling with saliva. "Kind of. I like to have fun. You guys used to be fun, too. Now you're all business-y and relationship-y. Yawn."

"You were so embarrassing last night," Abby said. "Everyone in the Valley is talking about you right now. I don't want to be a part of it." She was shaking.

So was I, but for different reasons. "Enzo didn't seem to think so," I said, but before I could finish, the last few things I drank the night before had chugged their way into my mouth in a violent spasm. I opened my bag and barfed into it.

"You should go," Norah said, with the most disgusted look on a face I'd ever seen. "You're not well."

I closed my bag, which stank, and wiped my mouth with the back of my hand. I took a sip of Norah's water, swished it around in my mouth, and spit it into my bag.

They all looked like steam might blow out of their ears. We'd been friends for ten years, each one of us a Napa Valley transplant, here to live some sort of dream. We partied, hard. But somehow, I was the only one who didn't get the memo that the rules had changed.

I shivered in my seat. "I'm not well, guys," I whispered. "I'm really not."

They'd never seen me cry—I wasn't a crier. I didn't take anything seriously enough to cry over it. But this was terrifying. I couldn't lose them. I needed to do whatever it took to win them back.

"Tabitha, we know," Serena said. "You need professional help."

She handed me some cards with doctors' names on them.

"No, I mean, yeah, I do. I could do with some talk therapy maybe? But what I'm saying is that I'm sick."

"What do you mean?" Abby asked.

"I have cancer."

I threw that out there like I was tossing a turd into a punch bowl.

It shut them up, though.

I spent the next hour explaining to their stunned faces my diagnosis, my prognosis, my action plan. By the end, we were all promising to do better, be better friends, talk more, drink less.

Within a few days, we shaved my head. I launched into an intricate playbook that was harder than any job I'd ever had.

They never asked me what kind of cancer I had.

CHAPTER
SIXTEEN

I SMELLED IT FIRST. The smoke.

If I'd been writing a wine description, I would have called it *"caustic, woodsy, with soaring overtones of acridity released from actively combusting vegetation."*

The smoke smell wasn't from the incense Krista and Ben had left behind. That was more of a *"whiff of sandalwood on the top note, carried forth by a deep base of oud and palo santo, dusted with u breath of clove spice."*

I'd put that out just to be sure.

I stepped outside, and it was clear that there was a fire in the wilderness. A few deer dashed past.

I couldn't see it yet.

I wondered if it would be the last thing I saw.

Nobody knew I was here. Who would tell the girls if I burned alive?

The weeks had been good to me here. I was sober at that point and feeling mildly hopeful.

I didn't know if I was ready.

Was anyone ever ready?

The possibility of a wildfire's taking me out was a possibility

I'd eagerly signed up for. Here it was. And for the first time in my life, I needed to follow through on a promise.

A solid decision. I congratulated myself on good adulting.

The lights flickered and then died.

I heard the roar of what must have been a backup generator, and everything powered back up.

The exterior sprinklers had engaged.

At least this magnificent house might survive.

My first steps outside the house were shaky. My stomach wobbled.

I took deep, long breaths in the hope that perhaps smoke inhalation would kill me first. The thought of my skin burning frightened me. But I kept going.

Smoke inhalation didn't seem to be doing the trick. I'd smoked so much, my lungs were probably soaking it all in like two briskets.

Memories battered me like flashes of lightning: Serena's laugh when I'd imitate her exes. Sunday mornings recovering with the girls in our ugly kitchen. Once being part of something called a "Dream Team."

But these memories were tainted now. I'd lived a wasted life. Never applied my talents to anything worthwhile. Sold wine, wrote about wine, drank wine. Lied. Deceived. Sabotaged. Was abandoned, quite rightly.

This is fine, I thought, stepping deeper into the darkness. Like that cartoon dog.

I heard animals scurrying and crying out, their voices strange and distorted. What does a deer sound like when it's panicked?

You don't want to know.

It occurred to me that I hadn't called 911.

Fuck.

I was the only one up here. It had to be me. If the fire department could put out some flames that might save animals, then I needed to facilitate that if I could.

Then I would at least go out doing something for others.

Reluctantly, I turned to go back to the house.

The smoke was thick, and I was disoriented, lost in the woods, directionless, ready to give up and die.

I didn't realize how hot a wildfire would be.

I thought about sitting down.

I'll never know if what happened next was caused by the fire, a coincidence, wrong place, wrong time—

I heard the splintering, then the crack. When I looked up, I saw a branch the size of my dining room table right before it hit me in the face.

WAKING up was the second-strangest experience of my life.

Again, a smell. Pungent. Powerful.

Bombards the nose with notes of animal hoard and unfolds on the palate to reveal layers of rotting chicken, Bikram yoga studio, and aged headcheese. Pairs perfectly with wet garbage and thousands of maggots squirming in slow motion.

It didn't matter that I'd opened my eyes; it was pitch dark. Couldn't see a thing.

I was cold. Ish. It was hot somewhere, but not where I was.

My face was swollen; my nose pulsated with every heartbeat. It hurt when I touched it.

I was also being cuddled by something. It was holding me like a doll. I was stroking its fur. Coarse. Thick.

"Where are you from?" I remember saying before realizing I was inside my own water tank, being gently rocked back and forth by what can only be described as a sasquatch.

Because

that's

what

it

was.

I was in and out of consciousness while being babied by a North American forest-dwelling primate with an arresting case of body odor.

My water tank was empty from the fire hardening. And the fact that the pump had been off for a while.

He must've found me lying in the forest and brought me here to wait out the fire.

My head throbbed; my ears pinged.

The sasquatch treated me delicately, which must've been a struggle, because this thing was built for power. I could tell from how its body felt—sturdy, solid, smelly—and that if he decided he was done with me, he could snap my head off my body like the tail off a shrimp.

But he didn't. For however long we were in there, he held tight (not too tight) and hummed, a low thrumming sound that either created my soporific, stunned state of being or was the perfect complement to it.

I was frightened, totally, completely, and thoroughly. I felt like a small animal yanked out of her natural habitat and put in a cage for transport. Or like I was a kitten handed to a child to play with against my will. Things were happening to me that I had no frame of reference for.

Was I—a pet?

Was I dinner?

A plaything?

Terror vibrated in my bones. Waking up inside a concrete silo while a fire raged around my home was unutterably horrifying.

Waking up inside a concrete silo in the arms of a mountain monster was not on my bingo card.

Hours. Days. Years. I still have no comprehension of how long we were in that water tank together, fire raging all around us. The memories of it don't feel real—like a dream. Everything that came after still feels as real, although it's less believable by a lot. But something happened between us in that tank. We bonded. Without speaking a word.

I couldn't see his face, but I could sense his worry. And it wasn't only about me, though I was touched by how he was committed to making me feel better. His family was on his mind, and he was conflicted about them. It was as if he was telling himself he'd done the right thing by picking me up, that his family knows what to do and they would survive. He was worried that they were worried about him.

Either he was speaking to me telepathically or his vibes were easy to read or I had somehow transformed into a superempath as a result of a serious bonk to the head. I felt more attached to him than I had felt to anyone or anything, and the depth of my feelings—which came on instantly, like a spark—was miraculous to me.

Whoever had decided to make bigfoot a big furry cartoon character, a muppet, a riddle, got it wildly wrong.

This thing was a god. Primal. Intelligent. Capable of surviving almost anything.

Eventually pulled me out of the top of the tank like he was one-handing a baby out of a womb. So strong. He took great pains to ensure he didn't scrape me or bump my head on the hatch, maneuvering me around as if I was a prize in one of those claw machines.

When we finally emerged, the area around my home was unrecognizable.

Let me be clear: whatever those two crazy, mutilated crypto kids did to fire harden this house was top notch. It survived the flames like a boss. I lost a window or two. There was some smoke damage. But it was still in good enough shape for anyone to live in.

I could see down the mountain to the highway. And although the redwoods remained, fire-loving guys that they are, nothing else did.

The beast carried me across the patio and to my back door as easily as lifting a loaf of bread from a shopping cart. He left me inside.

I didn't make a fuss about his leaving the door open. He was, after all, raised in the woods.

He also laid me down on the floor, which was fair enough. He didn't know about beds, either, probably.

He disappeared.

Starving, concussed, and ready for a hot bath, I stood up, slowly, to survey the damage.

I was so weak, all I really wanted to do was lie back down on the floor and, well, die.

This would've been a great time for that.

The smoke that lingered in the air strafed my throat. I turned on the tap—nothing. No water was left. I'd need to turn the well pump back on, but I wasn't ready to deal with that yet.

I desperately wanted to call my friends.

Thrice I'd tried to die, and thrice I'd failed. I couldn't do anything correctly.

Every ounce of confidence had drained from me and was replaced with a chasm of loneliness.

I walked to the front window and looked out over my kingdom of scorched earth, wondering how this was going to get worse.

CHAPTER
EIGHTEEN

THE GALS and I had a bat signal. Anytime one of us texted an emoji of a bat to the group chat, we were to drop everything and rush to the house of the person who'd sent it.

It was 7:05 p.m. on a Thursday when we got the signal from Serena.

We were all standing around her kitchen island by 7:45, sharing a bottle of Screaming Eagle, and I was wondering what we were about to celebrate.

Truth was, I was a tiny bit annoyed that Serena was stealing my thunder. I'd thoroughly relished being the center of everyone's attention for the past several weeks as I battled my illness so bravely.

"Except for the hair," Norah once said, "you'd never know you were sick."

But sure, whatever. If Serena got promoted to married or found her birth parents, then I guess we could take a break from my needs for one evening. The wine was unbelievably good, so I didn't have many complaints.

I picked up the bottle for a refill.

"Are you allowed to drink?" Abby whispered. "On your meds?"

"Doctor said it's fine," I said with a wink.

I needed to change the subject.

"Alright already, Serena," I said. "Why all the hullaballoo?" I was already tipsy, so this came out as "hullowbawlooh."

She took a deep breath. "I'm glad you're the one who brought this up," Serena said. "I'm going to be leaning on you quite a bit, Tabitha."

"What's going on?" Norah asked.

"There's no easy way to say this," she began. "I had a mammogram last week. And they found something."

The room went squiggly as the gals dabbed their eyes and hugged and gushed about how much we loved each other. How together we could beat the cancers that plagued our friend group, and love conquers all or something like that, blah blah.

We were there for what seemed like hours. Multiple bottles were opened, and I partook in each one, getting sloppier and sloppier. She had a schedule for chemo once a week and radiation every day for six months. We'd take turns driving her. We'd take her to the salon to shave her head, like we'd done with me several weeks before.

"We'll host a fundraiser," Abby said. "With all of our contacts, we could easily put together a wine auction or golf tournament to give you a little breathing room financially."

"I feel sick," I said involuntarily.

"Oh, Tabitha," Abby said, turning pale. "We can include you too, of course. We assumed that with your trust fund you were OK. But maybe that's not the case?"

This had gotten completely out of hand.

I excused myself to go to the bathroom, where I looked at myself in the mirror. Hair was nonexistent. I touched my pale scalp it as if seeing it for the first time. What had I been thinking? Why had I done this? I had no plan. No endgame.

Did I do all this for attention?

What in the ever-loving hell was wrong with me?

I walked back to the kitchen slowly. Time was up.

My throat caught as I tried to say the words.

"Tabitha, what is it?" Serena asked. "You look like you saw a ghost. Last thing I need now is for my house to be haunted."

"I—"

"It's OK," Serena said. "You don't have to talk. This is probably retraumatizing you. Have some water. Have a seat."

I stood frozen to my spot.

I had to find a way to get the words out. It was now or literally never.

"I have to tell you all something," I began.

They all turned to me, their faces concerned.

"I—I don't have cancer. Never did. I made it all up."

Their faces didn't change as I succumbed to big, heaving, feel-sorry-for-me sobs. As if I was the victim in this scenario.

They continued to look at me as I fell apart, until Norah took a step toward me and placed her hand on my shoulder. She looked deep into my eyes and said:

"Now why don't you tell us why you've been lying to us for weeks."

The three of them exchanged glances and began to cackle like a coven of witches.

Was this a sting?

Serena was fine. She'd made the whole thing up.

"How long?" I asked.

"How long, what?" Serena shot back.

"Since you've known," I said.

"From nearly the first minute you said it," Norah said. "We were all crying and carrying on at that lunch, but you never cracked. You let us leave there thinking you'd convinced us you had cancer. I thought you'd admit it when we took you to get your head shaved. But I've got to hand it to you. You don't quit, do you?"

"There's a darkness in you," Abby said.

"I—"

"No, no," Norah said, holding a finger up. "You don't get to talk. You had us running errands for you, buying your groceries. You were calling us in the middle of the night to talk about your pain and your worries."

"I dropped you off for chemo!" Serena said, pounding her fist on the counter. "I saw you slip out the back and call an Uber."

"Say something," Abby said.

"Norah told me not to speak," I said.

"Here we go," Norah said. "Jesus, Tabitha. Were we not paying enough attention to you? You get all the attention! All the time!"

"We think you have an actual mental problem," Serena said. "It's called main-character syndrome. You believe you're the star of your own movie."

"And you don't realize there are other people in the cast," Norah said.

"Do you know that since Serena made her fake announcement an hour ago that you never once asked her how she was feeling?" Abby looked livid. "Or how you could help? You kept drinking her wine, though."

"Priorities," I said in a sing-song voice with a fake smile.

"It's not funny," Norah snapped. "You're legitimately a bad friend, have been for a while. But you're clever. And you pay for things sometimes. No harm. No foul. We knew our relationship with you was thimble deep."

"Really? I thought we were—"

"We weren't," Serena said. "But we felt sorry for you and were amused by you. And now this? We can't continue. Won't continue."

"I'm blocking you from all my socials," Abby said as she whipped out her phone.

"I've already done that," Norah said. "Blocked your number from my phone, too."

"I will be doing all of that as well," Serena said. "Now kindly exit my home."

"Please, guys," I said, once again centering myself in the drama. "How can I make it up to you?"

"Oh, my god, Abby," Norah said. "Do you remember when she swallowed all those vitamins so she could make herself throw up?"

They were talking about me like I wasn't in the room. And that was one of my tricks. Never take B12 on an empty stomach unless you want to boot all over the floor.

"Oh, and how she made labels to put over other people's prescription bottles to make them look like they were hers?" Serena chimed in. "Classic."

I'd spent hours digging through people's recycle bins in search of pill bottles. I thought that was clever. Shout out to my neighbor Mario Garcia, who was really going through some stuff. Most of my bottles were his.

"You never lost your eyelashes or brows," Norah shrieked through laughter. "What kind of chemo spares your facial hair?"

Then, Abby: "She told us, 'Oh, that's normal for some people.' And she thought we believed her!"

Serena could barely speak she was laughing so hard. "You—you never told us what kind of cancer! We waited and waited. Would this be the day? Or this? You're a writer. Make something up."

Norah continued: "You didn't know this, Tabitha, but we all went into Queen of the Valley Hospital and talked to the lady at the information desk. We told her what you were doing. She'd text us every time you came in, with *'Here she comes. And there she goes.'* I can't wait to tell her we busted you."

"Stop, guys," I said. "It's enough. I get it."

"That's another thing," Serena said. "We've all known each other for, what? Ten years now? Have either of you ever heard Tabitha say 'Please'?"

"What are you—?" I was stunned. I had good manners.

"Never," Norah said. "Anytime you ask for something, it's

'Bring me groceries, all organic' or 'Drive me here.' Rarely a *please* and never a *thank-you.*"

"Or a *sorry*," Abby said. "She never says she's sorry. Ugh, you guys. We've been saying it for years. She's toxic. Not chemotoxic, though."

They were laughing so hard, tears were streaming down their faces. I thought Norah might choke.

"Toxic? That's harsh. I'm sorry. Sorry about all of it."

"Sorry you got caught is more like it," Serena said. She walked to the front door and opened it. "Now get the fuck out of my house."

I stepped over the threshold and shivered against the cold on her front porch.

"Abby?" I took one last shot with the nicest one.

"It's time for you to take yourself back to whatever redneck swamp you crawled out of, OK?" she said. "It's over."

"Enjoy your fiancé's business cottage," I said to Serena, one last dig. "Did he get you a ring yet? Or does that come after you complete your onboarding?"

"And call an Uber, will you?" Serena said. "You're too drunk to drive. As usual."

CHAPTER
NINETEEN

I DIDN'T CALL AN UBER. I walked. Or stumbled, rather. It was about a three-mile journey in the dark to the Victorian. I tried to smoke, but the cigarette hit me pretty hard, and I fell into a bush. I lay there longer than I should have, looking up at the night sky, unconcerned about whether a neighbor might see me. I didn't think I could get up.

I was home by dawn, sitting in my ugly kitchen, sobering up. Humiliated. Bald for no reason. Searching my mind for an explanation as to why I behaved this way, coming up with nothing.

And even if I understood my own behavior—that I was traumatized and acting out—what good would it do me now? I'd lost everything.

What was it they'd said about main character? I Googled it, and hell if that didn't describe me to a T.

I'd lied about cancer, for fuck's sake.

But then again, so did Serena.

Stop.

The Napa Valley fog hadn't lifted yet that morning, but the Valley had been awake since before dawn. Not like I'd been awake, still coming off a night-before bender. It was late August, and the harvest workers were picking; trucks filled with grapes groaned down the highway; and I was tired of living.

I'd moved here several years before to work with wine, and I didn't love it. Don't get me wrong; I loved wine. My purchasing power single-handedly kept the Napa Valley wine industry afloat. I didn't like working, though. I was bad at it because I didn't need to work to live.

As I watched the men and women in the early hours of that morning, working harder than I had in my life, I realized something very important.

I was nothing.

I did nothing.

I had nothing.

What was I even doing?

No weapons in the house. Nothing stronger than some Norcos I had left over from a dental procedure a few years back. (I took them, of course.) I didn't hate myself enough to endure the violence of slashed wrists or a slit throat.

There was only one possible way for me to off myself that morning.

I got in the car and drove to Devil's Punchbowl.

———

Hidden on private property in a town called Angwin, Devil's Punchbowl is a round basin at the bottom of a waterfall filled with clear, cold water. It's exactly the kind of place one loves to know about and hates that others know about it, too. It's also a perfect place to drown. A body could be in there for days, for sure. But it wouldn't be quick.

After dawn, I stumbled down the unsanctioned trail clearly marked NO TRESPASSING and stood at the banks of Devil's Punchbowl. Gazing into its surface, I became acutely aware of a missed opportunity to re-create the famous painting of Ophelia. If only I'd worn a beaded silver gown and brought a bouquet of posies. As it was, I was still wearing the jeans and sweater I had on the night before.

"Oh, well," I said. "I won't see it anyway."

I scavenged a few stones and put them in my pockets. As one does.

I set my keys on a boulder. I didn't care who ended up with the car.

"Here's mud in your eye," I said, as I jumped in feet first. Or something like that, I'm sure. Deeply philosophical last words.

The cold slammed into my body, and I felt as if I were being sliced to bits. A momentary panic, a flinch, a spasmodic lunge toward the shore to save myself.

I stopped, if only because I knew that if I got out now, I'd have to drive myself home in my freezing, wet clothes and I'd probably die of hypothermia anyway.

Release.

The quiet enveloped me and I realized how much I liked it. When was the last time I'd been immersed in silence? At work, I bounced around talking to people all day. In the car, I sang with the radio. At home, the TV blared or I was on the phone looking for the party.

As my extremities grew numb, my thoughts began to feel as if they were things I could touch. In the silence, I felt overcome with the total me-ness of me. Not in the main character way my former friends had accused me of, but as a real human being. I was a life that existed. That breathed. Wanted things. Slept. Yearned.

No acting.

No performing.

No clever clown show to humiliate myself before anyone else had a chance to.

It was only me and my thoughts in this soundless void. Me and my body full of poisons.

I could get used to this. I felt great.

And like the newborn babe yanked from the warm, squishy

environs of its mother's womb, I found myself similarly snatched from my amniotic reveries.

"What the hell do you think you're doing?"

I pulled my face out of the mud with a satisfying *schluck* sound to see a man in overalls looming above me.

"Did you not read the no-trespassing signs?" His dog, a wiggling Australian shepherd, barked at me. I wanted to bark back, but I didn't have the energy.

The guy's face was a shade darker than crimson, and I had to assume he was the property owner or something because of how enraged he was. Nothing I could say would make the situation better, so I got up and walked slowly, like a zombie, to my car, as he yelled about rule breaking and danger and private property. I don't remember grabbing my keys, but I obviously did that.

The dog gave chase, nipping at my ankles as it tried to herd me. The man called out, "This is our drinking water. No swimming!"

In my replays, I call back to the man, "No one goes swimming in a sweater and jeans. I still have my shoes on. Great observation skills, Einstein." But I'm done embellishing stories. After you've been through what I've been through, the unvarnished truth is enough.

The dog managed to grab a chunk of the back of my thigh, and the bruise bloomed purple, then blue, then sea green over the course of the next two weeks as a reminder of how I'd failed.

I looked in the rearview mirror. I was blue. I was shaking uncontrollably, my body juddered so hard I thought I might crack my teeth.

I desperately wanted to go home, but I knew I needed medical attention.

I guess I wanted to live?

None of this made any sense to me—and I was the one making the decisions!

There was a hospital in Angwin, right nearby, but I kept driving down the Silverado Trail to Queen of the Valley. I figured, if I had to be in the hospital, I'd rather be with the hard-partying Catholics than the no-drinking, no-meat-eating Seventh-day Adventists.

But the joke was on me. I was treated for hypothermia and released in six hours.

I didn't bother letting anyone know.

In the next three weeks, I packed up and moved to Del Norte County, which is where our story continues.

One of the first pieces of mail I would receive at Kevin, forwarded from the address that my car was still registered to in Napa, was a citation for trespassing and a parking ticket from the City of Angwin.

It was still sitting on the kitchen counter.

THE SMOKE SMELL would never go away entirely, I learned. And neither would my new friend.

He'd simply—pop up. I'd become inured to his scent. I would never see him coming, and I lost track of him when he was leaving. But that, I guess, is one of the superpowers of the sasquatch: hiding.

I expected Dick to come by, and he did. He scolded me about turning off the well pump and told me who to call about getting power restored so I could get off the generator. He filled me in on all the information about the fire that I had been unable to get. It had been set by buddies of Murphy Grundlage, who hoped to get revenge by smoking out the squatches and blasting them all out of the world like a sinister game of Duck Hunt. He'd blown off his own arm with a homemade pipe bomb, like a dumbass, and they blamed the bigfoot. They were caught and will be punished. I thought the whole thing was seriously fucked up because they knew I lived there. I was one of the last people to see that guy alive.

"Tell those dummies I expect an apology," I said.

"You could take them to civil court," Dick said, "but they ain't got a pot to piss in between them, so it might be more headache for you."

Dick made a good point. A lawsuit against a couple of locals wasn't on my to-do list, so I filed the thought away.

Before Dick left, he brought in a few cases of wine and some Cheez-Its, which was a thoughtful gesture.

Nary a peep from Annie.

Everything changed after the fire—like the lingering smoke smell and the fact that the forest looked like the surface of an uninhabitable planet: black with piles of ashes, some of them still smoldering. Deer covered with black soot. Trees creaking under the weight of dead limbs. Vaguely volcanic it looked.

And the sasquatch, of course.

I'd be melting some Velveeta on the stove like a true foodie, and I'd look up to find him standing there. Next to the island. Looking at me as if he was trying to tell me something.

It would be silly for me to tell you that he was tall. And hairy. And malodorous. Redundant to say that his feet were quite large, and his face apelike. You know all this already.

What you miss from the caricatures, the carvings, the lowbrow keychains and stickers, and the cheaply produced late-night documentaries is how it feels to be in the presence of something so commanding. He was thoroughly in tune with the environment in which he lived. He existed with the rhythms of nature, not over it like a human, which I think is what gave him the ability to move through the world like a ghost. His power was natural. Like the trees around us and the understory under us, he was, in every sense of the phrase, a part of this place from the dawn of time.

Every moment I was with him, I felt myself changing. I understood the smallness of humans, how our tiny brains could never comprehend the profound intelligence of a creature like this. Instead, we hunt it, shoot it, run from it, mock it, turn it into a meme.

No wonder I was hell-bent on a path of self-destruction that left carnage in my wake. I was a dumb human who'd forgotten—

or never knew—that powerful mysteries guide us if we can only let go of our creepy little want, want, wanting and instead wake up to the magnificence of life on this earth.

I was a small thing who thought she was a big thing but really was no-thing.

And it wasn't all learning to dance to the music of the spheres and connecting with my inner ancientness. We had some fun, too.

I never once said it aloud because it was too hilarious, but I called him Meatus in my mind. His member was as big as you'd expect, and it just—swung there between his legs with the tip poking out of the hair every so often. It was the size of a doorknob, pink and weirdly nonthreatening. He would always be Meatus to me, even though this was a bit of a backslide into my old ways. Probably should have named him something dramatic like Gravitas or Robert, but Meatus is what stuck.

I had recurring dreams of geoducks. Surely, that's unrelated.

Meatus watched me do everything—from washing dishes to making breakfast, lunch, and dinner. He loved scrambled eggs and hated nachos with Velveeta. I'd say the names of everything I did, and I could see that he was registering language. He never said anything back.

He also didn't laugh, which was OK. I didn't make too many jokes anymore.

I was learning a new love language.

He brought me plants to eat, and I ate them all. I have no idea what they were. I put salad dressing on some greens once, and I thought he was going to lose his mind from joy.

"All that over a foraged salad?" I asked as he grunted, beat his chest, and banged the Heath Ceramics salad bowl on my dining table made of reclaimed wood. "It's literally Paul Newman Vinaigrette."

He was adorable.

So adorable I never thought to ask him if he was responsible for tearing the previous owners to shreds.

I'm not sure I would've liked the answer.

CHAPTER
TWENTY-ONE

I WAS FEELING PRETTY good for the first time in a few weeks. Not great, mind you, but mildly less distressed. Knowing that I actively wanted to die—three times—and then failing left me with a strange hollowness at my core. I was devoid of hope, unable to envision any kind of future for myself. The juxtaposition of those desolate feelings with the daily grind of simply surviving after trauma gave me the sensation of existing outside of time, the community, the world.

But Meatus made me if not happy, then at least curious about something. He came around one afternoon and, ever the good sport, let me put him in the soaking tub. It was one of those Greek-style numbers, tiled all over, and you stepped down into it. He plunged in, excited, without much prompting on my part.

Warm water was a revelation for him, and he seemed content to bob around in there for most of the afternoon, letting me do whatever I wanted.

Krista had left behind an assortment of creams, lotions, potions, and unguents that together were probably worth what I made my first year at Voltaire.

I thought about the girls as I chose a fresh cedar-scented body wash from one of those artisanal Brooklyn brands owned by some polyamorous husband/wife/wife/husband team that wants to *"redesign the way we wash, for our children's future."*

We loved this kind of thing unironically.

Abby would buy three bottles—one for herself and two for gifts—and if she liked it, would sell it in her store. Serena would post the packaging on her creative ideas Pinterest page. Norah would complain about the price ($150 for eight fluid ounces) but buy it anyway and then refill the empty bottle with something cheaper and put it in her guest bath.

I allowed Meatus to have a sniff and made a motion to let him know what I was about to do. The warm water seemed to have lulled him into an agreeable, mellow mood, so he didn't mind a bit that I was lathering him up with the *"finest essential oils and saponification elixirs from artisan-owned farms and intentional greenhouses."*

Judging from the weird grunting, kind of like the sound a pig makes when it figures out it can scratch its own back on a fence, Meatus liked himself a spa day.

For a guy known for his feet, he seemed to come alive when I soaped up his hands.

"Lots of pressure points in there," I said. "Press here when you have a headache." I pressed lightly at the base of his thumb. He sank into the water and sighed.

Ten points for Tabitha. Giving to others.

After the bath, Meatus let me spray him down with a leave-in conditioner. (*"Fortified with dandelion essence and a superfood complex of rare fruit, fresh herbs, and pulverized seeds for enhanced thermal protection and frizz prevention."*) While I was combing it through, he popped the top off and drank the whole thing. Then he threw the bottle on the floor and made a face.

"I know, I know," I said. "It's vegan."

It took about an hour to dry him. My only regret is that I had no way to photograph him.

Because he looked astonishing.

Have you seen those photos of blow-dried cows? How their fur puffs out all over?

Obviously, his hair was longer, but that's what he reminded me of.

He couldn't stop looking at himself in the mirror.

I was a wet, sweaty mess next to him, so I decided to shower up and take a dip into Krista's wardrobe to make things nice.

I chose a beige cashmere sweater and a soft pair of pants, probably bamboo fibers or something equally esoteric. That case of wine was still in the kitchen from when Dick had come by, so, what the heck, I thought.

We sat on the sofa together, two good friends having a normal one. Turns out sasquatch enjoy chardonnay—in case you were wondering. He was drinking it by the bottle.

I did my best to keep up.

I remember making eggs and dropping them on the floor.

I remember laughing and Meatus grunting as we ate them anyway.

We cuddled on the couch. I braided some of his hair. He scratched behind my ear like I was a puppy.

The last thing I remember before I blacked out was trying to teach him the Macarena.

Then, a lot of darkness and muffled sounds. Some movement. Like someone dropping a camera into a backpack with the record button pressed. A kind of jumble.

The following morning, I peeled one of my eyes open at dawn to catch a glimpse of Meatus outside, twisting around on the ground and rubbing himself on trees.

Guess he was afraid the others would make fun of him if he rolled up smelling like he'd wandered out of a GOOP convention.

I quickly got up for a hair of the dog, tossed it back, pulled a sasquatch hair out of my teeth, crawled back under my sheets, and slept until the afternoon.

BRIEF INTERLUDE

I invite you to find quiet space and read this next section aloud for full effect:

Oooh, no. Omigod. Omigod.

No. No. No. No. Oh, no. Oh, no.

Oh, goddamit. Oh, god. No.

Please, oh, my god, no.

No. No. nononononono.

No. This didn't. NO. No no no. Dear sweet Jesus, no. shitshitshitshitshitshitshitshitshit.

No. This can't. No.

Ohhhhmmmmagaaaahhhhh. No. How? Oh, god. Oh, no. I should call someone.

Oh, god, don't do that, you fucking moron.

What a fucking nightmare.

Oh, my god. I'm a disgusting freak. I'm a freak. A freak.

Oh, wow. They're gonna sell tickets.

I might be sick.

Bworp.

Bworp.

Oh, no. Oh, never. This. I can't. Oooh. Wahhhh. Ooooooo, god.

Whywhywhywhywhywhywhy did I? How? What the hell is wrong with me?

Oh, my god, all of them were right. I'm vile. Foul. A fetid, sweating beast, unhuman.

Disgusting. Unlovable. Oh. Oh. Oh. Gawd.

No. Ohplease Ohplease Ohplease.

Tell me this didn't— This can't be. I didn't. I couldn't. There's no way. I didn't do.

Oh, no, I did. Yes, that is definitely. Yep. Yessir.

Oh, you've done it now, Eggs. Holy mackerel. Good lord. Oh, god. I did. I really did.

No way. No way. Oh my g—

TL;DR: I fucked the samsquantch.

BRIEF INTERLUDE

It was a guy in a costume, right?

BRIEF INTERLUDE

No. It wasn't.

BRIEF INTERLUDE

Welp, there's no coming back from this.

TWENTY-TWO

WITHIN DAYS of my unholy union with Meatus, vomiting overtook me, swift and relentless. None of the usual descriptions of barfing—like boot, hurl, retch, upchuck—come within a million miles of offering an adequate description of what I experienced. Volumes of liquid, chunks, blood, parts of organs (presumably) were being forced out of my body, up my esophagus, and through my gaping cakehole with the force of a fire hose. The pain was so overwhelming that I barely (barely!) was able to point the jetsam issuing forth from my darkest regions toward the toilet. I had to go outside.

This.

Lasted.

For.

Days.

I broke a rib. Maybe two.

I was dehydrated. Dry as a bone. Crud formed in the corners of my mouth.

Meatus found me somewhere on the property, face pressed into the sooty earth, covered in a substance so alien and so vile that when I smelled myself, the heaving would begin again.

He took one whiff and ran back into the charred forest, leaving me there.

I thought I would die in that spot, wherever it was.

Finally.

As the spasms overwhelmed me again and again, I called out for death himself to come and get me.

I must've passed out—probably had done so several times—because when I woke up, I was back inside my house, still covered in filth, and looking up at Meatus, who was holding a dead possum by its tail.

This would make a heartwarming Christmas card, I thought, wishing that Meatus understood humor. And holidays.

I had only a moment to reflect on how a life of survival in the forest could make one more serious than someone who grew up with a trust fund and now lived in a house with radiant floor heating, because, yet again, I was gripped by a powerful, irresistible force.

I lunged for the possum, yanked it out of Meatus's mitts, ripped its head off, and ate its warm brain raw.

I pulled a writhing nematode out of my teeth and swallowed it, too.

Then I peeled off the possum's gray pelt, dropped that on the floor, and sank my teeth into the animal's flesh. Way more blood than should have been inside a creature so small bubbled out of my mouth, dribbled down my chin, and pooled in my suprasternal notch. It formed a pasty consistency anywhere there was soot, and I was c-o-v-e-r-e-d in soot.

As I ate the last bit of chewy/crunchy pink tail (*the grisly texture belied its toothsome appeal*), I realized that something was terribly wrong with me. The only things I didn't eat were the feet. I don't know why.

Oh, yes, I do. The tiny toenails squicked me out.

I shot a dramatic look that was meant to convey the phrase "What the actual fuck, Meatus?"

He understood.

He walked over to me, took the sticky possum remains out of my battered hands, and dropped them on the floor.

Then he placed his hand on my abdomen.

I stared at him, stunned beyond comprehension.

He nodded.

And I knew.

I was knocked up with a sasquatch baby.

Meatus seemed pleased. As pleased as he could look.

I, on the other hand, was a feral, psychotic, raging beast-creature, slathered in blood, soot, snot, dirt, and vomit. Bugs. So many bugs. Everything itched. My entire body swelled and throbbed and ached.

I left Meatus standing in my living room, which was now splattered with possum guts, mud, and other miseries, and I stumbled to the bathroom, leaving a trail of filth behind me.

The mirror was terrified of what it saw. Leaving the sheer volume of grime aside for a second, I had noticeable jaw muscles. My eyes glowed in a shade of amber that, had I not looked absolutely unhinged, would have scored me a modeling contract. My teeth seemed longer, pointier somehow. My boobs were massive and thoroughly untouchable, the pain was so severe. And smells. I could write a whole chapter on smells. Mine and others I sniffed.

Tears left tracks in the smut, but I didn't feel them. I felt everything—and I mean everything in the universe—except my own tears.

I wasn't pulled together, but there was nothing to do except go back to Meatus and figure out what came next.

And what came next?

The doorbell rang.

CHAPTER
TWENTY-THREE

HALF OUT OF MY MIND, but clear enough to know that anyone walking in on this scene would call the police, I made my way to the door.

The doorbell rang again.

Then, knocking.

I threw a glance into the living room where Meatus had been only a few moments before. I didn't see him, so I assumed he'd slipped out the back and into the woods in that way that he had.

"Coming," I said to whoever was on the other side.

"Tabitha Eggs?"

"I'm coming," I said, a slight edge in my voice. What if they wanted to come in? My house looked like a crime scene and smelled like a Civil War hospital.

I cracked the door slightly and said, "How can I help you?"

"Tabitha Eggs, you've been served."

The guy shoved an envelope through the opening in the door, and I caught it.

"Have a nice day," he said.

I felt a low growl form in my throat. That was new.

I released a sigh of relief that he had left, even though the right thing to do would have been to mention that he has a small mass growing on the bottom lobe of his left lung, and he should get it checked out.

I could smell it.

I could hear it munching away at his healthy tissue.

I made a mental note to find out who he was after I got myself sorted. It's not his fault he's a process server. Folks gotta eat. Telling him about the tumor, which was now exceptionally tiny (but ravenously hungry) would be an act of service.

Is this how sasquatch worked? Was I getting some of that bigfoot power from the fetus? Because if this was only a fraction of the sensory information a full-blooded sasquatch could obtain from its environment, it's not surprising at all that we haven't definitively found them. This was otherworldly.

I tore into the envelope, and it was indeed notification of a lawsuit that had been filed by dead Krista's niece, claiming she is the rightful owner of the property at 10101 Tule Elk Way and ordering that I vacate the premises or face criminal consequences.

This was the last thing I needed today.

I picked up the phone and rang Annie.

Her number had been disconnected.

"Bitch," I muttered under my breath.

I stepped outside onto the back patio after going through the living room, which looked more like a butcher shop than my magnificent home. I lifted my nose into the air and drew in a deep breath through my nose and mouth.

Meatus was still in the area, close by, possibly in some kind of bramble, like a blackberry bush. Dick was standing at the counter of the general store, selling some chewing tobacco to a person who smelled like dirty jeans. In the car driving by on the highway below, a child was eating Goldfish crackers. His mother was angry. His stepfather daydreamed. His baby sister was sleeping, and when she awoke, she would scream in pain from teething.

Annie had left town. Her scent was nowhere in the area.

Not that it mattered.

I had to laugh. After all my big talk and big dreams, here I was, in a ruined home that I'd apparently stolen and on the brink of being a homeless single mother to—something?

Is this how karma worked, because, good one, universe. I'd made a mess so monumentally huge, you could see it from space.

A wave of nausea ran through me, and I braced myself for the coming spewage by walking farther into the woods.

But before the fluid came up, I had the urge to release another growl, and it echoed through the trees.

I turned around to find Meatus.

He'd dropped a bundle of berries and a dead deer at my feet.

I dropped to the ground and shoved all the berries, thorns and all, into my face.

This did not faze Meatus.

I kept going. I sank my fingernails into the soft abdomen of the deer and devoured her internal organs.

Except one kidney.

I offered it to Meatus and he swallowed it in one gulp.

Look at me, learning to share.

TWENTY-FOUR

NOTHING TO BE DONE about being evicted. I didn't have a legal leg to stand on. I barely had a leg-leg to stand on.

My body wouldn't let me do anything but gestate.

I was alone most of the time, save for Meatus's feedings, for which I was grateful. I could tolerate only raw, recently living meat-food without succumbing to heaves so powerful they pulled my muscles and snapped my ribs.

My body was unrecognizable—bruised and swollen.

I don't know how much time passed. I was the size of an eight-months-pregnant woman, albeit one who looked like she'd been swallowed whole and shit off a cliff. And my hair had grown in, down to my shoulders, in thick, jagged hanks, the texture of a hanging rope.

It was pure white.

And eyebrows. And eyelashes.

White.

I was the crone in the falling-down house in the woods. Don't come too close, or she'll boil you into a stew.

The Meatus fetus squirmed constantly, and it was strong—I had hematomas on the outside of my abdomen from what felt like roundhouse kicks. My hips felt like they were being forced apart by a massive speculum.

A front tooth was loose and bleeding. My mouth was full of sores. Other teeth were chipped. If I were to survive, I'd eventually need a set of implants.

I showed the loosest tooth to Meatus. I gingerly touched it, waggled it slightly, and started to sob.

He picked up what I think was a deer rib and crunched into it like it was a rice cake.

He motioned to me to do the same.

The sasquatch understood that I needed calcium. But there was no way I could crush a deer bone in my mouth with a full set of *working* teeth, much less with the horror show that was happening in my mouth at that time.

I couldn't do much but lie on the floor surrounded by blood, bones, and offal—and moan.

The experience was a psychedelic trip gone pear-shaped. There were times I believed I must've been poisoned or had accidentally eaten a metric ton of psilocybin or something.

Aside from my extraordinary sense of smell, which informed me of everything—from when the ferns in my yard were sporing and what part of the forest Meatus had walked through on the way to my house, I had visions.

I could see and understand most of what Meatus was thinking by the visions that appeared in my head, and I became convinced of how nature is an unimaginably vast network of plants and animals communicating, working together, surviving together, sacrificing, giving, and sharing.

Humans don't have a clue.

We're deeply unsophisticated.

The only reason we're as "advanced" as we are is that we're willing to do things to nature that nature isn't willing to do back.

I saw colors I'd never seen before. Whole spectrums of light danced around me all day and night. I felt and smelled and heard energy emanating from the trees, the birds, water, clouds.

And the sounds? Everything makes noise. Osmosis has a pitch. Soil purrs. Leaves whisper secrets. Seeds underneath charred forest conspire with one another. Animals talk. All the time.

Sprouts are joyful. Roots cheer one another on. The canopy? Chatty, like a bunch of old ladies in a nursing home.

The sun has a sound. It hums and smacks and pops.

The moon emits a tone so soft and sweet, it can lull you into a trance.

Such exultation swirling around us, and we are asleep at the wheel.

There's a whole separate thing happening out there, and we aren't included.

We're small.

My questionable choices, my terrible friendship, my selfish pleasure-seeking were inexcusable, and I needed to experience the regret that came along with them. I needed to do better. In this state, I realized what it was that I was really after, and it wasn't forgiveness or absolution—even though those things would be nice. I needed to shift my energy to be more aligned with the power of nature.

I'd never wanted anything more. I expressed these feelings in thought to Meatus, as he cradled me that day. He seemed to feel pity for me, the tiny human in his arms who couldn't take care of herself. I accepted his pity and his love as he chewed deer bones into a pulp and spit them into my mouth like I was a newborn baby bird.

CHAPTER
TWENTY-FIVE

BECAUSE I WAS BEING EVICTED, I stopped worrying about the condition of the house. Perhaps if my situation had been different, I would have called my dad and gotten a pit bull attorney to defend my claim to Kevin or at least attempt to reclaim some of my ever-dwindling trust fund.

As it was, shit got really weird.

I was in no condition to speak with humans.

Or speak, full stop.

I thought in English, but my mouth was incapable of forming words. I could grunt, moan, scream, shriek, grumble, growl, howl, and bark. But I couldn't say my own name.

My living room had become a boneyard, slick with the blood of forest animals and piled with gnawed-on bones. The Nancy Meyers kitchen transformed into a Michael Myers wet dream.

I needed to bathe, but I didn't care. I probably should have put on some clothes. Didn't care. I definitely should've called someone, literally anyone, for help.

Didn't care.

Had the seasons changed?

Didn't know.

I'd taken to sleeping on the floor of the bathroom. The tile felt good on my burning skin, and somewhere deep down, the human that was still left in me knew it was better to barf into a toilet. I had that going for me.

A sunny day. They happened, but the sunlight rarely made its way to the forest floor, so thick were the trees even after the fire. I was awakened by a sunbeam in the skylight. I peeled myself off the floor and crab-walked to the patio to see if I could catch it. Bask in the rays if only for a moment.

And there, in the sunbeam, was an egg.

It was nearly fifteen feet tall and made of stones, all stacked neatly together, solid, as if they'd been mortared together.

But they hadn't.

I touched it, and it was immovable.

What a wonder.

I turned my nose up and sniffed the air, taking in the information from the scents.

He'd done this. Several trips. Painstaking work. It had taken days.

Had I not come outside in days?

It was, without hyperbole, the most beautiful thing I'd ever seen.

I leaned in and wrapped my arms around it. Love radiated from it and engulfed me.

I was loved.

The baby kicked.

I stayed there for hours, months, an eternity, as the rocks introduced themselves to one another and giggled at their predicament.

TWENTY-SIX

I NEEDED TO FEED, but I was alone. Food was close. I could smell it, hear it, feel it.

I tuned my hearing to the forest, and the forest knew I was on the prowl.

Baby steps off the back of my patio turned into confident strides.

Confident strides eventually gave way to a hybrid bear crawl that felt more efficient for hunting.

The scent of charred wood, singed duff, and all the other chemical processes left behind by a wildfire competed with my attempts to lock onto my prey. So did the forest.

It knew what I was up to, and it was braced to defend itself.

"Over there," the forest whispered. "Over here. Behind that. Beyond the other thing."

But it was lying. The soil, the leaves, the bark, stones, and seeds were trying to protect my prey.

The voices were cacophonous whispers, diverting me, taunting me.

"Don't look there. Look here. No, look there."

Nature can be a creepy bunch of school kids messing with you.

The tactics worked until I felt something shift—a palpable

click or flip of the switch. I was able to turn off the noise and home in on what I wanted.

He was beyond the ridge, nibbling on some sprouts.

He sensed my coming, but it was too late.

I launched onto the elk's back, wrapped my hands around his antlers, and snatched with a force I did not see coming.

His neck snapped and we both collapsed to the forest floor.

"Feed! Feed!" the forest urged, as if it hadn't, moments ago, been trying to trick me.

I tore into the still-warm carcass and feasted. Every bite made me more famished than the one before, and it was only after its eyeball burst in my mouth that I had a conscious moment when I remembered who I was.

The vision hit me like a sneaker wave. I could see what the stag had seen, which was a white-maned, starving creature leaping at me, nubby little fangs bared, panic in its eyes. I could feel what it felt, the day it was born (curious), the day it mated (powerful), its first sight of its twins (disconnected yet satisfied).

I'd crossed the Rubicon.

I was feral.

I thanked the elk for its sacrifice as I tore its muscles apart with my hands. I ate until I heard the bacteria arrive. Whether they floated in, attracted by the powerful chemical process, or whether they woke up and caused the powerful chemical process, I didn't know. Their hungry chatter, along with the wispy comments carried along by fungal spores, was enough to let me know it was time to go.

You won't find a main character in the forest. Everything here is either living or dying and there's no in-between.

I'd never felt more at home.

CHAPTER
TWENTY-SEVEN

I WAS ALONE when labor started.

I'd have been furious if there'd been a single moment to process what was happening.

The first thing I noticed was that I couldn't smell as well, and colors, lights and energies dimmed.

I didn't know what was happening.

I panicked.

I lumbered out to the back patio and tried to howl, but only a weak, scratchy sound issued forth.

The pain sneaked up on me, aggressive and certain. Like a blow to the back of the head with a lead pipe. Only a split second to register before you succumb completely.

I made peace with the idea of dying. It's what I wanted anyway, and now that I'd seen the truth about the human impact on the world—and my dumb, unserious contributions to making everything a little bit worse simply by existing—I thought it might be best for everyone if this is what killed me. My only regret was that I wouldn't be able to see the gals' faces when they learned I'd been found dead with a sasquatch fetus in my belly.

That would have been wild.

But no. Turns out I needed to cook the little guy for only a few weeks before he was ready to join the world.

Waves of excruciating pain nearly sent me out of my mind.

I couldn't remember how I'd gotten here, who I was, or why this was happening.

My blood mingled with the piles of dead animals in my house, and my screams were weak—like those of a human woman again.

I didn't bargain or try to talk the universe out of it. I simply bore down, endured the agony, and waited for death.

One huge push—the one that broke every blood vessel in my eyes—and a furry, wiggling, baby-thing slapped onto the polished concrete floor.

We encountered each other briefly, each of us equally surprised to see the other.

He had his father's eyes.

I wanted to grab him, snuggle him. But I couldn't move. My body wasn't much more than a bruised and swollen meatbag.

"Meatball," I called to him. He responded to my voice with a slight tilt of the head, as if to say, "That's not what I thought you'd sound like."

He was about the size of a full-grown French bulldog, covered with goopy fur, and he was howling.

I made the mistake of peeking down there after I pushed this thing out. Big mistake. I was torn to shreds. For days, every time I stood up, blood and fluid would run down my leg. I walked like I was trying to hold a football between my knees.

I don't know how much time passed before I moved to pick him up. I pulled him to my breast and felt his heartbeat against mine.

This was love.

This. This was it all along. We weren't laughing or swapping stories. We weren't busy trying to one-up each other or show off. It was simply me and my Meatball, absolutely mad about each other.

He squirmed loose and clambered to the door.

Did all sasquatch babies run around on their own on Day One?

"What is it?" I asked.

He looked up at me.

He shit on the floor.

"That's OK, buddy." Did I need diapers?

The gravity of this situation was beginning to hit me.

I had made that with my body. That magnificent creature HAD GROWN INSIDE ME AND IS NOW SHITTING ON MY POLISHED CONCRETE FLOOR.

He clawed at the door with his sweet, tiny hands. I opened it, and he bolted into the backyard.

My baby had just hightailed it into a burned-out forest.

Was I a good mother or a bad mother?

I was a tired mother.

I sank back down to the floor and was overcome with hunger. For normal, human food. A salad. Some roasted squash. An apple.

As I was dreaming about a buffet, Meatball appeared in my doorway again. His muzzle was covered with blood. And a feather was stuck in the corner of his mouth.

"Oh, you were hungry," I said, as he climbed into my arms.

We both fell asleep on the floor.

It was as if I had emerged from a nightmare.

Into a bigger nightmare.

Meatball had pooped all over me and was gnawing on my wrist by the time I woke up.

He had a full set of teeth already.

How long had I been naked? The whole time? My god.

I scooped up Meatball and inched my way to my closet, where I found a robe and put it on, jostling him from one arm to the other so I wouldn't have to put him on the floor. I wasn't sure I could catch him if he ran again.

I wasn't ready to look at myself in the mirror yet.

Dizzy and half out of my head with anxiety, I emerged from

the bedroom, Meatball in my arms, to find Meatus standing in the living room.

Raw fear unlike anything I'd experienced gripped me.

I didn't recognize the look in his eye. Less curious. More determined.

I took a step back.

He was here for Meatball.

He reached out his hands toward me. He nodded his head as if to indicate we were in agreement about what he wanted.

I was not in agreement.

This was my child.

I shook my head slowly, no.

"Never," I said.

Meatus growled, and every hair on the back of my neck stood at attention.

He wasn't kidding around.

I knew he could rip me in half if he wanted.

Meatball made a few small squeaking noises. He didn't take his eyes off his father.

Meatus took a step toward us, and I ran.

Locked the door of the bedroom.

Locked the door of the bathroom.

Hid in the tub, shaking, while Meatus unleashed his supernatural strength on my house for what seemed like hours.

He was tearing at the walls and floors, howling ferociously. I heard the kitchen sink—the one I'd recently asked whether it was planning a trip to Rome—skid down the hallway after he'd torn it out of the counter.

Then, silence.

Why didn't he simply break down the doors?

Because we were friends.

The thought filled me with sorrow.

After dark, we emerged.

Famished.

My fireplace. My floors. My windows. The kitchen sink and all the appliances.

Everything that made my house a home had been destroyed in a fit of primal pique by a northwestern skunk ape.

Meatus wanted his son. His son needed to eat.

I wasn't equipped for any of this.

I stood there in a stunned panic, my mind racing with possibilities, all of which led to dead ends.

To whom could I go for help?

"We're on our own, kid," I said to Meatball.

I had a few cans of refried beans and a handful of odds and ends. We'd have to make do.

I was searching underneath piles of debris for the can opener when I heard it.

The sound was low and uniform, almost imperceptible. A deep hum, unlike anything I'd ever heard, even during my superhuman experiences.

It grew louder, deeper, more ethereal, surrounding us in a vortex of sound waves. I didn't dare go outside.

I could feel it now, a rumbling in my guts, a shivering in my spine. My organs readjusted themselves.

Meatball was transfixed on the window.

Surrounding the house, hundreds deep, an army of sasquatch. Their red eyes twinkled in the night. The smell was overpowering. My knees wobbled. I felt like I might retch from the intensity of the scent. Corporeal. Emotive. Sticky.

The entire house vibrated. The ground shook under me. Glass, plates, art, and books toppled to the floor, giving the carnage in every corner of the house an eerie, postapocalyptic quality.

I crouched with Meatball under the window, where they couldn't see us. My thighs burned. My crotch was on fire.

I was in no condition to handle this.

The unearthly tone continued until the sun disappeared from the sky, leaving Meatball and me in the dark.

Alone.

I thought about Ben and Krista. The memory of their twisted, shredded limbs shook me.

What were they capable of? What would they do when they realized I wasn't handing Meatball over? He was as much mine as he was theirs—more so.

But I couldn't possibly take on a family of sasquatch.

We had to run.

CHAPTER
TWENTY-EIGHT

I WASN'T willing to wait until morning.

Trying to figure out what to pack for us was utterly impossible. I needed lots of underwear, considering my prison pocket and surrounding tissue looked like someone had set off a Roman candle in there. I snapped up as many Restoration Hardware towels as I could find because I didn't know what Meatball's excretory needs were going to be. A jacket. A few blankets. My wallet.

That was it.

And I needed a shower in case I ran into people. The smell alone was suspicious.

As I scrubbed up with my favorite Flamingo Estate body wash, savoring the jasmine fragrance, I realized what was so astounding about my recent sensory experiences. Sure, I could smell everything. Every scent molecule that bounced off my olfactory nerve was carrying information. Information that I understood and could process. Unlike sniffing wine—or perfume or anything really—where you're evaluating the characteristics as good or bad, when sasquatch smell things, nothing is good or bad. It simply is. And you make decisions related to your survival based on the information.

No time to ruminate. The sting of the water on my shredded genitalia was enough to motivate me to move along. That and the fact that my toddler-sized newborn was eating a Tom Ford lippie.

Guess it really does take a village. Especially when your rug rat is a ravenous cryptid.

Aw, he missed me! After I towel-dried my hair and put on comfy clothes for what I assumed was going to be a long drive, he jumped into my arms and nuzzled my neck, leaving a streak of Cherry Lush on the side of my face.

"I love you, too, Meatball," I said. "Let's get you somewhere safe."

The surge of emotion in that moment was wholly new to me. I loved Meatball, but it was more than that. He was my calling. My heart's purpose. I experienced a soul-level understanding that my future was Meatball. And I would stop at nothing to protect him.

Love, as powerful a word as that is, barely touched my feelings for my baby. His earthy smell, his inquisitive eyes, his sweet little feet—the combination had ensorcelled me. He was mine and I was his and those were the only truths I knew.

I ferried him to the garage. The humming had ceased.

But no car seat.

Was I really this bad at this?

No. No, I wasn't. I'd been in a primal fugue state for at least a month, maybe longer, and it wasn't like I could send Meatus on a jaunt to Target in Eureka to get baby stuff. I needed to drive and not worry about things that would work themselves out.

Meatball took to the front seat and the seat belt way better than I thought he would. I think it's because it happened so fast.

As I piloted the Benz down the road, past the place where the branch had hit me and where all of this had begun, Meatball started making a noise.

That low rumble sound. He was letting his family know —something.

Where were they? I scanned the woods for signs of a gang of sasquatch. Nothing.

They were there, though. I could feel them watching.

I had to hurry. This was madness. I wasn't sure of anything—only that I could not, would not, give my baby over. Not now. Not ever.

On the verge of a psychotic break, I pulled into the parking lot of the general store. I waited for the customer before me to leave. Then I went in and got Dick.

"Oh, Tabitha," he said. "Have you been sick? Is that a wig? Your hair. Your teeth! What happened to your eyes? What the—"

"Something like that. I need you to send your calls to voice mail, close the store, and come with me, please."

"But I—"

"Now." I said this with enough urgency that he grokked the importance of what I was asking.

A few moments later, Dick was standing on the passenger side of my car, staring down at Meatball.

"He's a beauty," he said, breathlessly. "What a magnificent creature."

Then, "What are you doing with him? This is not good."

I explained as best as I could. Convinced Dick I wasn't stealing Meatball, that he was, in fact, mine.

He took a deep breath. Rubbed his chin.

"What're you expecting to do now?" He asked.

"We're on the run, Dick. I can't stay. I can't fight this. They're coming for him, and they will take him."

Meatball had pulled everything out of my glove box and was playing with my emergency flashlight.

"Wait right here," Dick said, and he walked back into the general store.

I needed to get going. Dick was taking so long that I got back into the car and turned it on in case I needed to drive away.

He emerged from the shop.

I pointed to my wrist. He waved me off.

"I don't know if this is helping or if it's hurting," he said. "You seem hell-bent on getting out of here with your hybrid. You're probably going to fail. There's no hiding him. Not permanently. But until you can get yourself sorted, take yourself to this address. Imma call ahead to warn them. They'll help you."

I took the business card from him. "F.I.G.S.," I read aloud. "What is this, Dick?"

He looked over his shoulder to make sure no one was listening in.

"Can you keep a secret?"

The answer to that was decidedly no. I didn't keep anyone's secrets, ever.

"Of course," I lied.

"I need to swear you to secrecy."

I motioned to Meatball. "I don't really have time—"

"It means the Fellowship of International General Stores. It's a secret society of people like me who help people like you when they're in trouble. Go to this address. There will be assistance for you there. No judgment. Just help."

"Is 'F.I.G.S.' a biblical reference or something?" I asked.

"We figs things," he said. "Couldn't find a word that started with X that would work with the acronym."

"Whoa. That's clever, Dick."

"I'm worried about you," he added.

My eyes filled with tears. "That means a lot to me. I haven't been a very good friend to most people. I'm touched that you worry. And I'm so scared."

"Call me when you get there. And don't show him to nobody. For me, none of this ever happened. Right?"

"Right, Dick. And thank you. Let's figs this."

And we were off to a town called Lookout in the high desert of Modoc County, about a five-hour drive away, out of Fort Dick, through southern Oregon and back into California.

CHAPTER
TWENTY-NINE

SUGGESTION: Playing the following road trip tunes while reading the next section will enhance your enjoyment of reading about our adventures on the road.

Carry on Wayward Son by Kansas.

That's it. That's as far as I got because holy Christ on a cracker, it's impossible to enjoy a road trip less than twenty-four hours after you've given birth to a cryptid/human hybrid.

I could barely sit, my nether regions were so swollen. I was bleeding from my—wherever—for hours. I didn't know what to eat, and I didn't know what to feed *him.*

Meatball, having been alive for less than a day, found existence wildly fascinating. Everything he could reach went into his mouth, which made it hard to steer, especially when we got onto the rising, curving roads that led to the heart of the high desert.

I was busy wrestling from Meatball's shockingly strong fist the Chanel hand cream I keep in the glove box when the blue lights flashed.

My brain left my body. It disappeared. I became a shell of a human—nothing but a body and nerve endings. Meatball swallowed the small tube of hand cream whole, and I didn't have the time or the energy to freak out about it before the officer shone her Maglite into my blood-red eyes.

I handed her my license and registration before she had a chance to ask for it. Meatball seemed to know something was up, and he sat in his seat, under his seatbelt, patiently.

"I'm sorry, officer, was I speeding?"

"Yes, ma'am," she said, finally taking the spotlight off me and making notes. "What's the hurry?" She looked at my license. Then at me. "You change your hair?"

I didn't even think about the fact that I no longer looked anything like my driver's license photo. Time to deflect.

"It's my dog," I said. "He's sick. I'm not from around here. I'm desperate to find a vet."

Meatball was sniffing out of the window, his primate face pointed away from the officer.

"What kind of dog is that?" she asked, her nose wrinkled.

"Rescue," I said. "Not totally sure, but he was special needs when I got him and he has these weird seizures—been seizing all morning and I'm out of his medicine, but my grandmother is sick in Modoc and I'm on my way there and I don't have cell service out here and I don't know what to do."

I still had the ability to lie while looking someone straight in the eye. If you keep talking, they'll do anything to shut you up.

Within the next five minutes, Meatball and I had a police escort to Klamath Falls, where the officer wished us well in the parking lot of Klamath Pets 'n' Stuff.

"You get that little fella taken care of, and we'll forget about your speeding," she said. "And you might consider getting a new license photo because you look so different now."

"Um—"

"You look good," she said, unconvincingly. "But I really had to squint to see you in there."

"Thank you, officer," I said. "We really appreciate it. I've been through some stuff."

"I hear that," she said. "What's the precious angel's name?"

"Meatball," I said.

She frowned.

"The shelter named him." I shrugged like, *Whatareyagonnado?*

She waited while I hoisted Meatball, who had somehow grown from French-bulldog-size to Lab size in twenty-four hours, out of the car and shuttled him into the waiting area of the vet.

He was heavy. I thought I might split in half lifting him. How was he growing so fast? How long had we been on the road? Was this normal?

None of this was normal.

I waved to the officer as best I could as the door shut, ringing all kinds of bells and causing the receptionist to look up at what we were doing.

Meatball started hooting, a low, huffing bark. We didn't have much time.

"Can I help you?" The receptionist asked. She held a finger up to her lips and pointed at a candle. The sign read, "When this candle is lit, someone is saying goodbye."

That hit me like a mop in the face. I wanted to get out of here before encountering some poor soul who had to put their dog down.

"Do you have a bathroom?" I stage-whispered without turning around. "We've been on the road for hours, and I'll check in, but I'm dying to pee."

"Through that door," she whispered, and I hustled us through, stepped quickly past a confused vet tech, and spirited my half-squatch baby out the back door.

I learned from faking cancer that there's always a back door.

My pain was excruciating, I was bleeding through my pants at this point, and both of us were weak, tired, and crabby.

I was in Oregon, for god's sake, the GPS having taken me on this wild route, and I wanted to get back to California as soon as possible. But I did what I had to do.

Drive through was our only option. I thought perhaps there'd be a time when some milk would come in and I could somehow breastfeed my baby, but it never happened. I'm not sure I could have tolerated Meatball's teeth anyway.

Chicken nuggies would have to do.

Meatball held one up to his nose, smelled it, and proceeded to devour the entire lot and the packaging and then wash it all down with a large Coke.

"You didn't even try the Jackass Sauce," I said. I handed him the packet. "It's got five spices." He ripped it in half, licked the packet clean and swallowed it.

Don't judge me. I was new to parenting.

I promised I would do better once we got where we were going.

As usual, though, I hadn't really thought it through.

CHAPTER
THIRTY

FIRST STOP in the high desert: Modoc General Store.

I pulled into the parking lot.

A man came out to greet me.

"You Tabitha Eggs?"

"Yes, sir," I said, too tired to be witty.

"Dick told me all about you," he said. "Glad to help you. Name's Mick."

"There's a whisper network of general store owners that helps people with problems too big to handle on their own?"

He thought for a moment. "He told you about F.I.G.S.?" he asked. "Dick must trust you. Generally speaking, those who run mercantiles or goods suppliers knew a lot about the comings and goings of people in town, out of town, and through town. We have a quiet understanding that we can use this information for good or for evil. Most of us choose to use it for good."

"I like the cut of your jib, Mick," I said.

"I've put together some items you'll need. I'll start a tab. Pay later. That the little fella?"

Meatball was asleep, full of fried poultry and corn-syrup-pepper sauce, and he looked adorable. I stroked his ear.

"That's him. Barely born and we're on the run."

Mick wouldn't let me lift a finger. Put everything in the trunk of my car, handed me some keys, and gave directions to his "hidden" cabin.

"Nobody's going to find you up there," he said. "And I keep secrets. Stay as long as you need. Pay what you can when you can."

I couldn't believe how nice he was being. "Thank you," I said, choking up. "I truly don't deserve this. Thank you."

"That's enough of that," he said. "Between me, Dick in Fort Dick, Rick in Barstow, and Chick in Reno, we've seen our fair share of human/cryptid shenanigans. It's part of the gig. Get on home and settle in before dark. My number's next to the wall phone."

———

The cabin was small, tidy, and remote. Meatball was still sleeping when we arrived. I put him on the sofa and covered him with one of the many sheepskin rugs. I needed to light a fire before the temperature dropped, but first I unloaded the car.

Lifting Meatball was one thing. It was my life's duty, my gift to him. When I carried him? No pain. I couldn't rustle up the same effect for groceries.

Slowly, painfully, I brought small loads in, one by one, until the car was empty, and I thought my uterus would squirt out of my vag, slither down my pant leg, and die in its own juices on the floor.

Mick. Dick. These two kind men in a weird secret society. They saved me.

Diapers.

Baby food.

Raw steaks.

Frozen veggies.

Cans of soup.

An absolutely enormous package of maxipads.

Mick wasn't kidding. He knew exactly what he was dealing with.

I went inside to shower and change.

Water pressure, good.

Lots of hot water.

Fluffy towels.

I curled up on the sofa next to Meatball. I pulled his odd little body close to mine.

He was developing a strong smell. Mercaptan. Sulfur. Onions.

Just like his daddy.

There, in the high desert, secreted away from everyone and everything I'd ever known, suffering the most comprehensive pain in my life, I sobbed myself to sleep thinking first, about the kindness of these strangers, who understood enough about what I was going through to include maxipads—and second, how I didn't deserve any of it.

CHAPTER
THIRTY-ONE

THE HIGH DESERT is a whole mood.

I can see the appeal for a certain kind of person. Nothing to challenge the eye. You could watch your dog run away for five hours out here.

But also: altitude. And if you're a person who hasn't spent much time in high-altitude areas, the transition can prove difficult.

I learned about altitude sickness. Y'all, it's real.

I was already having to learn how to walk without moving my vulva, but throw lightheadedness, nausea, vomiting, and diarrhea on top of it, and you've got a recipe for a miserable Tabitha.

I fed Meatball from the supplies Mick had provided. He loved it all, if I'm being honest. Kid never saw something edible—or non-edible for that matter—that he wouldn't happily shove into his gaping maw.

Food wasn't really the problem. I mean, it was. But something else was off.

To use a medical term, he wasn't "thriving."

When he was awake and not eating, he was scratching at the door, desperate to get outside. I had no way of explaining to him that it wasn't safe. I'd lost my ability to communicate with him. I tried everything—from repeating his grunts to attempting to speak with him telepathically, to howling. Nothing worked. It was gutting to watch him end up in frustrated hysterics every single day.

Every mommy wants her baby to be happy.

I was failing.

And utterly terrified.

My worry about Meatball's extended family taking him from me forever had morphed into a terror that I didn't know how to raise him.

I didn't know how to raise him, and he was suffering.

I called Mick.

"Clawing at the door, eh?" He asked. "I know you're a smart woman, Ms. Eggs, so I don't want to offend you when I say this, OK?"

"OK, Mick. I can take it."

"He's half wild."

"I'm not offended, Mick. I know this. What do I do?"

"He's half wild with something we'll never understand. And the half wild he is is primordial. Do you know what that means?"

"It means he's existed since the dawn of time."

"*He* hasn't. But *his kind* has. You're dealing with—I'm going to stop myself there because it's more than that. You are a mother to a being that you will never understand. You may love him. And both Dick and I supported your need to try to mother this creature on your own. And we wanted to save you from his family. You needed to know. But it's time to make some tough decisions. About your future."

"God, Mick," I said. "All I really wanted to ask was whether I should let him outside. Instead, you've plunged me into an existential dilemma."

"Let him outside then," he said. "He'll come back. He's being pulled by a powerful force. But you're still his mama."

I opened the door. Meatball bolted into the brush.

"I'm still your mama," I called after him. "Make good decisions."

Naturally, I fretted. Tidying the house, making a small dinner for one, doing a few loads of laundry—none of it helped.

As the sun set over the steppes that yawned away from my borrowed cabin, I heard the wail of a lost creature, yearning to go home.

MEATBALL CAME and went as he pleased. Within a few weeks, he was the size of your average NBA point guard.

I did virtually nothing but wait for him. Look for him. Think of him. Where could he hide out here, being that tall? Mick surmised that he'd been living in Modoc State Forest.

"Provides more cover. And more of what he likes to eat," Mick said. "Possible that there are more of his kind out there."

"Are they territorial?" I asked. "Or could he wander up and they'd be OK with him?"

"That I do not know," he said.

I worried more.

It seemed logical that Meatus was worried about his son, too.

It's not like the boy's father was a bad guy. We were friendly.

I loved when Meatball would come and stay for a while. Curl up in front of the fire for a few hours and rest. He let me pet his head, and my heart pressed so hard against my breastbone, like it was trying to go with him.

Most days, though, he left dead things on the back porch.

Hares, at first.

Then a few grouse.

I learned to skin them and eat them. It's what one does out here.

After a few weeks, though, the kills were bigger. The wounds grislier.

A headless raccoon.

One ripped-apart tule elk.

A great gray owl. That's an endangered species.

"He's acting out," Mick said when he came out to look at the piles of body parts on my porch. "He's not well. This is not the behavior of a healthy animal."

"Like those sad ones at the zoo that pace back and forth all day?"

"Exactly right," Mick said, dead serious. "If you love him, and you want him happy, you'll take him home."

"How?" I asked. "How?"

"Do you think you can get him into your car?" Mick asked.

I imagined this scenario for a moment. Communication was difficult, and he was so big now. I didn't think I could reasonably expect him to follow me. He wasn't a stray dog.

I told Mick what I thought. "I'm too small to do this on my own," I said. "He's going through a teenager phase. If he wanted to get out of the car, he would, and I would be unable to stop him. I could lose him forever.

"We're gonna have to do what F.I.G.S. has always done with large animals."

"What's that?" I asked.

"We're gonna have to knock him out."

THIRTY-THREE

I'D BEEN HEARING THINGS.

Rumblings, roarings, scatterings, splinterings.

Ruckuses so loud my human ears detected them.

I was seized with worry. Was Meatball out there trying to defend himself against an established colony of high desert primates?

That was the worst-case scenario.

Perhaps he was scuffling with other creatures. Coyotes and badgers. Wolves.

He'd never learned to hunt. He'd never learned to protect himself.

No one was here to teach him.

It's possible the sounds I was hearing weren't him at all. I'd never lived in the desert. Was he still alive?

What would you do if your child was wandering alone in the high desert?

I looked for him.

Day after day, I traveled a route of concentric circles out and away from the hidden cabin. With less than zero training in tracking, I scoured for footprints, snatches of fur on tree limbs, dead food, scat, anything that would point me toward Meatball.

I was desperate to see him.

The circles grew wider, and the days got longer. More and more, I was returning home in the dark, my feeble human eyes barely up to the task.

After one particularly daunting day when I'd discovered nothing more than a few scattered, sulfuric hot springs, I stumbled home through the scraggly brush, tripping a few times over roots and branches.

I'd gotten accustomed to my body being nature's punching bag. None of this bothered me anymore.

I heard the snap of a twig behind me. Ever hopeful, I snapped around and looked high, seeking Meatball's eyes.

I didn't see the coyote until it was attached to my leg.

I fell to the ground and lay still, grateful I had the wherewithal to understand this was a dog and if I shook my leg, we'd be playing a game I wouldn't win.

Its grip was vigorous and unstoppable, and the pain shot through me in lightning bolts, up my leg into every nerve ending. The animal growled and tugged.

I fought back tears and lay as still as I could. I cried out in pain involuntarily.

Big mistake.

The others came calling.

The pack circled around my head, snapping and growling.

I envisioned the girls getting the news that I'd been ripped apart by a pack of coyotes in the high desert.

"What a drama queen," Norah would say, rolling her eyes.

"If only she'd read the books I suggested," Abby would offer. "Coyotes don't feast on the enlightened."

"Play stupid games, win stupid prizes," Serena would add.

If I'd been a part of it, I would have offered something like, *"Exuding notes of terror and desperation on the nose, Tabitha made a fine coyote feast, revealing layer after complex layer of regret, shame, and remorse."*

I laughed to myself the tiniest bit. This shit was utterly absurd.

All of a sudden, I was overcome with relief. The coyote had released me.

Or rather, the coyote had been yanked off me.

Standing close to seven feet tall and smelling of the inside of a decomposing large intestine was Meatball. He was chucking coyotes into the desert like they were beanbags.

Then he carried me home.

I could feel his heartbeat in his chest, loud and powerful. He'd come into his smell, but I didn't mind. I buried my face in his fur. If I could have, I would have crawled right into him. Set up housekeeping next to his beating heart.

I had missed him so much and tried in vain to communicate with him—to beam my thoughts into his mind—on our clumsy journey. It wasn't like it had been with Meatus. Meatball was still a baby. Still learning how to be in the world. Still learning what he was and where he fit in.

His face was crisscrossed with scratches, and tufts of fur had been pulled out from all over his body. Was he fighting other creatures? Was another colony making things difficult for him? Was he doing this to himself out of frustration?

He was big—not as colossal as Meatus, but imposing. Any animal would have a difficult job if it tried to tangle with him. But surely there were tricks and tips he needed from his own kind? Training? Lessons? He was a baby running around by himself in the desert. I couldn't imagine the anxiety he must feel.

I was garbage for bringing him here.

When I awoke, I was outside the hidden cabin, a coyote's head tucked into my curled arm, its lolling tongue resting in the crook of my elbow.

I didn't want this kind of life for my son.

THIRTY-FOUR

THE BITE WAS BAD: two deep punctures and a variety of scrapes from where it was trying to hold on as it got yanked backward. Mick fixed me up with some kind of herbal home brew that stung, and he scored me some antibiotics to stave off infection.

"You had enough yet?" he asked.

"What was I thinking?" I asked. "Why did I run? He's out there fighting things and attempting to feed himself without any guidance. He's strong and courageous, but he's still a baby. He needs his father to teach him how to live."

"I'm going to agree with you on that," Mick said. "We know what you need to do to fix it. He'll be alright, but I think you need to get him home."

We made a plan.

Mick set up a gentle trap in the backyard, and I'd packed the car for a quick getaway. I needed to get back to Fort Dick before Meatball woke up from our ruse. I had no idea how he'd respond to being in the car now that he was so big. And wild.

I was adamant that no harm come to Meatball, and Mick agreed. It was a trip wire and only a trip wire, hidden enough for Meatball to literally—you guessed it—trip over. The idea was that he'd be on the ground long enough for us to jab him with a tranq dart filled with ketamine.

"You have ketamine out here?" I asked Mick.

"Wherever there are wild animals, folks have ketamine."

"I guess if it doesn't knock him out, we could always take him clubbing. Cure his depression."

Mick didn't get the joke.

We waited patiently, which was all there was to do. I tried to make light conversation, but Mick, like Dick, was a man of few words.

Then the sound of a branch snapping. Rustling in the brush.

I ran to the window.

Meatball.

He'd fallen to the ground.

"Got him," Mick said, grabbing the dart.

"No, wait," I said. "That's not where the wire is."

We bolted out the door to Meatball, who was lying on the ground, unconscious and bleeding from his head.

MY BABY! My darling boo. My sweet, sweet boy.

The gash was long and angry and dragged a jagged trail through his forehead and across the bridge of his nose.

"Get the first-aid kit," I said.

Mick didn't answer, simply got up, ran inside, and came back with everything I needed to clean up the wound.

"You want me to tranq him?" he asked.

"I don't know, Mick," I said. "What if it kills him? This is a head wound."

"What if he wakes up in the car?" Mick asked. "He'll be groggy. Won't know what's happened. He could lash out."

I couldn't take long to weigh my options.

"I'm going to drive, Mick. Let's get him in the car. He might be OK with it. I'm willing to take the risk. But give me the tranq dart."

I'd healed up a bit in the few weeks we'd been there, so dragging Meatball by one arm while Mick pulled with the other was terrible, but not as terrible as it could have been. At least I could do it now, even with my punctured calf muscle.

We closed him into the back seat, and when I saw how

cramped he looked, I ran back inside, snatched a pillow off the bed, and tucked it behind his head.

"Sorry about the state of the cabin," I said. "I tried diapers on him. Second-worst idea I've ever had. Take it out of my deposit."

"That won't cover it," he said. "How 'bout I send you a bill?"

"I'll make the check out to F.I.G.S.," I said. I blew Mick a kiss and drove away from the high desert forever.

CHAPTER
THIRTY-SIX

THERE'S something about having to pull off the road, climb into your back seat, and stab your nearly full-grown half-human son in the neck with a tranq dart that really puts things in perspective.

He had only begun to stir, the tiniest bit. I had to make a call. If he woke up and was angry or in pain and confused, he could lash out and kill us both.

I hated it. I hated myself for having to do it.

I hated everything I'd done to my darling boy.

This whole stupid thing was my fault.

Listen to your Aunt Tabitha, ladies. Don't let a sasquatch impregnate you. Causes all sorts of problems.

You'd never forgive yourself.

Back in Fort Dick after a journey that I am one hundred percent certain caused my hair to start falling out on its own, I didn't even stop at the general store. Even though I knew Dick must've known everything by now.

I couldn't go back to Kevin. I couldn't risk getting arrested or being discovered.

It's not like the place was livable anymore. I thought about the new owner, the niece, and how she'd be getting a destroyed house. I felt bad about that, but there was nothing more I could do.

Instead, I drove past my former refuge, up and around until the not-totally-unpaved road ended and the dirt fire road began.

I stopped the car.

Meatball was still honk-shooing away.

The only thing that made me feel better about any of this was that Meatball looked peaceful.

I took a long look at him. Memorized his features, which were decidedly apelike, but I could see hints of Eggs in there, too. His nose turned up at the end like my mother's.

I loved him so much.

But my love was killing him.

I gave him a sweet kiss on his fusty forehead.

Then I honked my horn and howled to the moon.

I felt the rumble in my feet first, the low vibration of a hundred ancient voices. When I felt it in my breastbone, I knew they were near.

I stood back and away from the car.

Their presence was unmistakable. I dared not move.

Meatball dreamed through it all. As his mother, I hoped he'd forget this chapter of his life. I prayed that the trauma he'd endured at my hands would heal, now that I had vowed to leave him be.

After a few moments or all of eternity, Meatus appeared. He looked at his sleeping son and then at me. His sad face shattered me.

How do you stay friends after something like this?

Short answer: you don't.

Meatus came to me. I backed away slightly.

He reached out his hand. I reached out mine.

Both of us cried. I'd never seen his tears before.

Then, before I even knew what was happening, he'd lifted

Meatball out of the car and disappeared into the depths of the forest—the parts that hadn't been scorched by human predators—where his kind lived peacefully as long as we didn't bother them first.

THIRTY-SEVEN

NO ONE ever came looking for me.

I should be dead.

But instead, Dick died. He passed away peacefully in his sleep. I found him.

The second-most-painful loss in my life.

We'd been roommates at the end. He once said I reminded him of his daughter. I apologized for that, and we laughed.

When he was diagnosed with cancer, I shaved his head for him. I nursed him through the worst of it all and let him go when the time came.

He trained me up and I became a full-fledged member of F.I.G.S. I manned the general store seven days a week. Spoke to Mick often. And Rick in Barstow. And Chick in Reno. Together we'd helped a lot of people—mostly domestic violence survivors. One time, I hid an escaped inmate in the storeroom. And in between all that, I sold cigarettes, lotto tickets, beer, sunflower seeds, and jerky.

I went by *Vick*.

In my store I took down any reference to forest primates. To me they weren't cartoons. Or jokes. Or prey to be hunted by incel jackholes looking for something to brag about.

If folks came in wanting to hunt squatch, I made them feel stupid about it, like it was the dumbest thing in the world. I'd send them to old Ferguson's Trout Pond instead, where they'd be guaranteed a catch.

If there's anything I wanted now, other than to die, it was for everyone to leave the sasquatch alone.

Someone moved into Kevin and fixed him up. That's all there is to say about that.

Oh, and you're probably wondering about Ben and Krista. I was very busy while all this was being sorted out, and I didn't have access to or care about news. I came to find out that they'd eaten what they probably thought was psilocybin and died right there in the woods. The dismemberment was blamed on coyotes.

Coyotes could really fuck you up. I knew that now.

Crypto dorks. Microdosing. Sad. But not mine to hold.

Serena breezed into the general store a few years back, bouncing a drooly, curly-haired baby on her hip. Asked me if she was headed the right way toward her Airbnb in Gasquet. Picked up some GoGurts and a box of wet wipes while her husband pumped gas.

My first reaction was to wave, to hug, to welcome her, to apologize again and again.

I eyed her baby (adorbs) and wondered if this connection could bring us back together.

My brain responded with an overwhelming NO.

Our babies weren't the same.

We weren't the same.

That chapter of my life was forever closed. The only thing I could give her today was a wild story to tell the others, and they'd all say I was lying.

I was done being a main character.

I didn't look her in the eye—not that anyone from those days would recognize me now. Long white hair, chipped teeth, Dick's old, baggy clothes. New name.

Before ducking into the back, I mumbled that she was our 100th customer that weekend and could have anything for free.

"Even the gas?" she said, ever the negotiator.

"Yep," I called back.

I watched her on the security cam, frowning at the selection. She didn't take anything other than the GoGurt and the wipes.

She was rich now and could be a snob if she wanted. My business wouldn't suffer.

I felt nothing. I'd atoned. No need to dredge all that up again.

At night, at Dick's house, which I'd named Harold, I sat in his rickety Adirondack chair and sniffed the air, listened for rustling.

I'd awaken to the occasional dead hare or a wild turkey left on the porch.

Shadows and smells. Sounds and movement. All of it triggered me.

I couldn't go back to society if I wanted. What would they make of me? How would I assimilate, knowing what I know now?

I'd wait forever if I had to. I'd stay here in this spot, my love brimming over and spilling out all over the forest. I wanted my love to be a beacon, a lighthouse that would bring him to me, to face me, to see me now, to know that I never forgot.

I wanted only to give him a glimpse of intense love that had built up inside me through the years and had nowhere to go.

Night after night, I called to Meatball, howling, grunting, saying his name. Sometimes I'd think I caught a glimpse, but sasquatch aren't seen unless they want to be seen.

No one ever snuck up on a sasquatch.

I waited in the forest, my new home, with the eagerness of a war mother—recklessly, endlessly hoping the one thing I'd ever truly loved would be the last thing I saw before I died.

ACKNOWLEDGMENTS

Many thanks to my wonderful support team of Meg Coogan, Kirsten A. Smith, Pamela Browning, Linda Shaw, Leah Eichler, and George Dondero. I'm delighted and relieved that none of you talked me out of this. Eric Raglin, your edits were superb and made the book better. And thank you to all of the small lit mags who have supported my projects along the way.

Like what you read? Please leave a review on Amazon! Support indie authors.

ABOUT THE AUTHOR

Bethany Browning is an indie author who lives and works in a redwood forest. She also writes cozy mysteries that have a lot less swearing than this one. You can find links to her published short stories at bethanybrowning.com.

Like what you read? Please leave a review on Amazon! Support indie authors.

BONUS CONTENT

HOW I CURED MY DEPRESSION
By Bethany Browning

The school nurse suggested I might have clinical depression, so naturally the first thing Momma did was take me to see her psychic[1].

"It's a demon," Miss Charlene said, too bluntly for my taste.

"It lives in the upper right-hand corner of your bedroom," She sucked a deep drag on her Newport. "Chicken feet. Big nose. It's draining your happiness like straw in a Slurpee." She waggled her fingers at me.

"Looks like *Strega Nona*?" I asked in all seriousness. "With a straw?"

"You're thinkin' of Baba Yaga, baby," Momma said. She tut-tutted. "Never should've let that Moldovan exchange student sit you that one time."

"I don't think so," I said. I knew what was depleting my life force and it wasn't no forest witch. It was a slit-eyed redneck boy named Road Rash what was giving me a case of the Mondays and I wanted him dead.

I knew better than to say that out loud. But then that backwoods mystic took a deep breath and stubbed out her lung dart. She took both my hands in hers, looked uncomfortably deep into my eyes and said, "Little girl, you're fixin' to be famous."

———

Here's what I knew about famous. My uncle had it once and died on account of it. My daddy wanted it now and he was willing to kill for it. And my momma said Daddy'd never get it on account of his weak chin and soft teeth.

Uncle Stoney was famous because he had a pit bull named Sluggo what could shimmy up a loblolly pine to fetch a flour cloth bag full of deer jerky. When he wasn't taking Sluggo round to all the state fairs and whatnot, he was on TV. Local. Regional. National. For about three years he and that pittie was everywhere. Johnny Carson had him and the dog on his Hollywood show three times, and I got to stay up late to watch it. Sluggo and him even went to Japan, where Uncle Stoney learned that the people who live there eat raw fish with sticks.

"You mean fish sticks?" I asked.

"Naw," Stoney said. "They call 'em chopsticks. Craziest thing you ever saw."

Then my Momma called him a Philistine and asked her how to spell it so I could look it up in the dictionary. She was right. Stoney, for all his glitter and glamour, was a full-blown Philistine.

But my point of all this is that my daddy's brother was right famous until his wife found out he was cheating with a woman who had a cat that could meow the theme song to *Dallas*. She slipped a crawdad[2] into his soup so his gullet would swell shut on account of his shellfish allergy. My beloved Uncle Stoney bloated up like a dead toad left on a hot road and dropped dead in front of the Frigidaire.

I wanted nothing to do with fame if that's what it brung a person. But my Daddy was another story.

How he planned to do that, I'll tell you in a minute. I got to lay a bit of track here first, so you understand where this story's going.

I was opposite. I'd had quite enough of folks looking at me and my general direction thanks to that knuckle-dragging pig fucker named Road Rash I mentioned before. What I wanted was to be left alone. For good. So when that clairvoyant looked at me with her dead eyes and said fame was coming for me, I was scared as if she'd told me a skunk ape laid eggs in my babydoll buggy. The demon didn't even register. I'd battled things worse than demons when my daddy was drinking.

It wasn't no picnic, Daddy rolling home at daybreak, yelling and screaming over me and Momma when all we wanted to do was to eat our Jimmy Deans in peace. He'd gotten physical a few times—including that day he'd thought it'd be hilarious to toss two bowling balls onto the trampoline with me[3]—and I limped into school worse for wear more mornings than I could count. Most kids stopped looking me in the eye, but Road Rash was on me like a shark that'd sniffed blood in the water. It makes sense now that I look back on it. All shit balls roll downhill and when you're under five feet, weigh seventy-five pounds and show up with a smashed face and cracked teeth in fifth grade, guess what. You ain't even left basecamp, baby.

Road Rash started with calling me Taterface and all that kind of nonsense. Flicking spitballs into my hair. Sticking his foot out into the aisle to trip over when I walked to the pencil sharpener. Sneezing my nickname. Knocking my books off my desk. Nothing too clever, on account of he wasn't capable of nothing that required imagination. He stuck to the greatest hits. The problem was that all the other kids piled on, too, and I was the unwilling center of their hostile attention every single day.

Depressed? You bet. After an entire school year of this, and getting whiplash from turning my other cheek, felt like I'd been eaten by a bear and shit off a cliff.

In the middle of all this stupidity Daddy discovered Jesus, quit drinking, and commenced to building an ark in the backyard.

"What's an ark?" I asked.

He launched into the most insane story I'd ever heard. God and floods and animals two by two.

"You believe that, Daddy?"

He said he did. And I said he'll believe anything, then.

"You wait, baby girl," he said. "I'll build this boat here for Jesus and then he will bless us with fame and fortune. People'll pay to see it."

I shuddered. Seemed to me that hundreds of animals crammed on a boat was a recipe for disaster. "Jesus don't need no boat," I reminded him. "Folks say he walked on water."

Then he said, "You're too young to understand." I disagreed, but I wasn't in no mood to explain to a grown man that you can't float all them creatures on a boat together. The gators alone would treat his good-ship-godly-pop like an all-you-can-eat buffet and that was before he'd even figure out where in all of South Cack-alackey he was going to find two tigers willing to share a cubby hole the size of a milk crate.

He got back to hammering, and I jumped on my rusty old bike. I'd heard there was demolition derby at the fairground and I was not trying to miss that.

There was no need for me to hurry. These derbies lasted all day long. But I was feeling wild and free, going as fast as I could, wind whooshing past my ears, taking my hands off the handle-bars to feel like I was soaring through the clouds. I was reaching my arms toward the metal beams that crossed the Black Creek Bridge at the entryway to the fairgrounds, when my flared hems got hanked up in my bike chain and I was hurled ass over teakettle onto the asphalt.

After I pried the pebbles out of the heels of my hands, and checked for traffic coming either way, I dragged myself—bike clamped on to me like a pitbull gripping a sack of beef jerky—to the side of the street, where that drooling meat bag full of stupid, Road Rash, was waiting on his own bike.

"Good one," he guffawed. "You're supposed to roll your pants up, dumbass."

I sensed that no help for me was coming from that direction, so I worked on unraveling this puzzle myself. It wasn't like it hadn't happened before. I wiggled loose, stood up and blew my bangs out of my face.

Road Rash glowered at me.

"You got something you want to say to me?" I asked. "Or are there not enough people around? No one to humiliate me in front of?"

He dismounted and dropped his bike to the ground. He had a look on his face I didn't recognize, cold, distant. Normally when he came after me his eyes twinkled.

I backed up.

He grabbed my bike in his grimy, freckled mitts. He hoisted it over his head like a trophy as he marched onto the bridge and tossed it over the side. He didn't even wait for the splash before getting on his own bike and pedaling across the bridge toward the demolition derby.

I looked over the edge at where she'd gone in. I'd jumped off this bridge before and I could maybe do it again. But right at the opening edge of summer some kid I didn't know had jumped—just like we all do—and had gotten murdered by a swarm of water moccasins. They attack in groups and are deadly. I waved bye to my bike and got on with it.

My pickle was thoroughly dilled by the time I walked all the way home. But there wasn't no time to rant and fuss like I wanted to—there was a TV crew at my house. And my daddy, getting interviewed by Leezay Quattlebaum of the Noontime News Team.

I stood there watching the whole thing and learned that if you hold your mouth open long enough, you *will* catch a fly. I spit it out, and my mouth dropped open again as I watched them wrap it up and pack everything into their van.

My daddy was about to bust out of his britches he was so

proud. I'd never seen that expression on his face before, and believe me, it was off-putting.

"Leezay says the story'll air at noon," he said, still grinning like he won a bet. "Tell Momma to make some pimento cheese sandwiches and we'll watch your Daddy get famous over lunch."

I did as I was told because I always did as I was told. Momma looked like she would die of embarrassment, but I'd seen that look before, so I knew what to do about it and that was keep my cake hole shut.

Until Leezay started her report, we three sat mutely, the only sound the mushy-moist chewing sounds of pimento cheese on white bread[4]. Then, disaster.

You think you know how ridiculous something it is until it's beamed into your living room at noon on a Saturday and a gaggle of hairsprayed, white-toothed know-it-alls make fun of it. Leezay had no interest in making Daddy famous for his building skills or his devotion to the Lord. He was the daily local moron, a laughingstock. And his ark? I'd only seen it from one angle. They showed the whole thing and I swear it looked like something a kindergartner slapped together with her tools for tiny tots.

"We have to move," Momma said, collecting our plates and throwing them in the trash.

Daddy stewed. I thought at one point I could smell his brain boiling.

"I think you should keep going," I told him. "Would Noah quit just because some haircut called him 'arking mad' on some second-rate Saturday infotainment show?"

He sucked his teeth. His face turned red. I knew this look, too. And I knew best to get the hell out of there.

Later that afternoon, after Daddy'd tied a few on, he stumbled through my bedroom door. The hairs on the back of my neck stood up. I could smell him from where I was sitting and I was on guard. Anything could happen now. And it had. And it probably would again.

"I need your bike," he said. "I'm out and your momma threw the keys into the backyard."

I hesitated to tell him what had happened that morning. He stood there, looking at me, waiting.

"I, uh—"

"Where'd you put it," he said, stepping toward me in a way that signaled he wasn't playing.

"It's in Black Creek," I said. "Under the bridge."

"Excuse me?"

I told him everything. How I tried to get to the demolition derby. The bike chain. Road Rash.

"Let's go get it," He rubbed his hands together like he'd just hatched a plan for a jewel heist. I reminded him about the water moccasins. And gators.

"Then let's go get Road Rash," he said.

I jumped up. "Yes, sir," I said, thinking about all the fun I was about to have when my drunk daddy unleashed on that human-shaped turd burger. "But you're gonna let me drive[5]."

———

Before we got to the bridge, I pulled Daddy's truck over to prove to him there wasn't no way I'd be able to pull it outta there. He seemed satisfied and jumped in the back of the truck.

"You don't want to ride up here with me? It's only a few more yards."

He shook his head no.

"All right then."

I maneuvered the truck into the parking lot. I could hear the sounds of the cars crashing, the announcer's high-pitched southern yawp and the crowd screaming. I loved it and wished I could stay. But daddy got eyes on Road Rash right quick. He was eating a sno cone that'd turned his lips corpse blue.

The crowd parted as my daddy marched toward Road Rash,

whose eyes were as wide as I'd seen them, which ain't saying much.

Daddy smacked that sno cone outta his hands and before anyone else could say boo, he'd wrangled Road Rash into a half-nelson and dragged him back to the truck, where he tossed him onto the flatbed. He climbed in behind him and banged twice on the tailgate.[6]

I didn't know what the plan was, but so far, I was having the time of my life. He banged twice again when we got to the bridge. I screeched to a halt because it was fun. Daddy looked pretty badass dropping out of the back, holding Road Rash in a vise-like grip, and dragging him to the guardrails.

"You throw my girl's bike in there?" Daddy had him pretty tight, but Road Rash continued to wriggle like a worm. He didn't answer.

A small crowd had gathered, probably followed from the derby seeing as the parking lot was right there. But no one stepped in to help. Says a lot about Road Rash, if you ask me.

I was having a high time, but then I started thinking about how Road Rash was going to take this out on me. And how when Daddy got riled up like this, sometimes he turned on me. By that time, I was having less fun.

"Daddy, put him down," I said, halfheartedly. There was a part of me that still wanted to see how far this could go. I'm only human.

"Put him down? You want me to put him down? All right, baby girl. You get your wish." He tossed Road Rash, screaming, right over the edge like he was a sack full of unwanted puppies.

I knew he could swim, but there was stuff in there that could kill him quick if Daddy'd picked the wrong moment to make a grand gesture. Road Rash splashed around in the current; I waited for the dreaded water moccasins to tear him to pieces, or for a gator to drag him under.

But just like most of my life, nothing happened, and everything turned out fine. I still didn't get my bike, though.

"We better go now," I said, and we both jumped in the truck and sped out of there like we was Bo and Luke Duke.

We didn't mention none of this to Momma. She'd find out something soon enough. Anyway, she was pretty dead set on moving after the shame Leezay Quattlebaum had leveled on this family.

Daddy disappeared into his drinking. Momma hid from him and refused to come out. And I was in my room, pacing. None of this was going to end well.

And what Daddy done might be funny to me. But it wasn't going to be funny to Road Rash. He was going to escalate, and I was terrified.

"Demon," I said, knowing how ridiculous this sounded. "If you're here, help me out. I don't want to deal with none of this alone."

And y'all aren't going to believe this, but the demon talked back.[7]

———

I felt pretty good the next day, all things considered. Daddy was already outside making a racket on his boat, and Momma had just sat down with the paper. It was like nothing had happened at all and I was pleased as punch to play along. It's what we did.

She looked up and asked me if I knew a Charles St. John.

I said, no ma'am I do not know a person by that name and why should I? She told me he was my age and that he'd gone missing after his house burned down. "Folks are calling him an arsonist and saying he run off."

"Let me see that," I said. And there he was, slack-jawed and squinty-faced, staring at me from the front page of the Burryville Bugle. Road Rash.

"Never seen him in my life," I said, sitting down.

"That's odd," Momma said, her finger tracing through the

article to find something. "Says here he's in your class." She passed the paper toward me. I refused to pick it up.

"Trouble remembering people, places and things is a symptom of depression. Maybe you should take me to a doctor, not a witch."

Momma started to defend herself, something about Miss Charlene and health insurance, when Daddy stuck his head in through the screen door. "Y'all seen my buzzsaw?"

"I'll help you look for it," I said, grateful to be freed from Momma's rant on how doctors don't know nothing.

———

Daddy was in a snit about his missing tools. Buzzsaw. Blowtorch. Flashlight. I didn't want to bring up the fact that he'd been drinking, but my mouth was working faster than my brain again.

"Maybe this is God's way of punishing you for taking up the liquor again," I said, and before he could take a swat at me, the cops pulled into the driveway with their lights on.

I froze.

Daddy took a more measured approach. His experiences with the police had not been positive. He assumed a defiant position. He spit.

The fuzz kept their distance, too. I think they weren't quite sure what to make of the giant contraption that looked not remotely nautical and wanted to stay back.

"We'd like to ask you some questions," the one with the big belly shouted.

"Go right ahead," Daddy said, not moving.

"Witnesses said they watched you toss a boy named Charles St. John off the Black Creek bridge the other day ago."

"Was that his name? We was playing," Daddy said. "You know how kids like to jump off."

The one with the big belly looked at the one with the long sideburns. Then back at Daddy.

"That's not how the witnesses said it went," he called back.

"That boy swam to the bank and crawled out. That's the last I saw of him."

"Someone says they saw your truck near his house the night it burned down."

"Not possible, officers," Daddy said, confident like he'd just won a trivia game. "I was too drunk to drive. You can ask my wife."

The officers looked at me. Did they think I was his wife? I nodded just in case.

Sideburns checked his notes. "We need to circle back," he said. "Y'all enjoy your day, now. And watch the beers. We may need to come back and ask some questions."

They got in their car and drove off. I ran into the bathroom to pee. I don't know what I would have done had they thought to ask me something. I would of spilled it all.

———

"Gator!" Momma yelled up to my room. "This is not a drill. Gator shot at the lake."

I bolted downstairs and the three of us jumped into the truck, me in the middle, and sped to the boat launch at the mouth of the man-made lake that Black Creek dumped into. Gator Day was my town's Christmas, and you never knew when it was gonna happen. You had to be ready.

Gators out of the water were always so much bigger than you thought they'd be. Even the young uns are the size of a Harley Davidson and the older ones are big as canoes.

I get reminded of this every Gator Day when some show-off kills one and drags it on shore. I think it's stupid, personally, to preen like a peacock over shooting something that can't shoot back, but I'm not the one in charge. At any rate, every time one of these rednecks blasts a ditch lizard in the brain, they hoist it up on a meat hook and slice it open from its throat to its tail. And every time, a whole bunch of mysteries get solved.

Golf balls, dog and cat collars, beach towels, laundry, small tools, children's toys—anything that looks tasty and unprotected is going to find its way into a gator's gullet. Every pet owner whose Fluffy or Fido went MIA comes to Gator Day and, likely as not, they find their fur baby's collar. It's closure, in a way.

I guess Road Rash looked tasty too. When they slit this one open, his slimy body slid out and slumped into a heap onto the pavement like that gator'd given birth to it.

And even though technically the gator was not part of the plan, I knew I could make it work.

The crowd gasped, just like in a movie. Everyone knew exactly who it was. He'd only been digesting for about forty-eight hours, so, other than the fact that he was sawed to pieces, he looked like himself. His eyes were a little livelier, though, I noted.

"Looks like that kid yee'd his last haw," I said, like I was new in town.

Chaos ensued. Tweedle-dee and Tweedle-deputy showed up. An ambulance arrived. Road Rash's parents had been notified and they came to ID the body, even though it was obvious. You could see that red hair from space. The real news team rolled up, too. Not that hack Leezay Quattlebaum. We got Bryce McGentry himself.

Nobody was paying much attention to the other treasures the gator's flayed tummy revealed. I thought it would be helpful to point them out.

"Hey, Daddy," I said. "Ain't this one of your buzzsaw blades?"

I could tell it was by the look on his face. And so could everyone else.

"And this?" I continued. "This looks a lot like your blowtorch."

"Sir, were you missing these items?" Sideburns was all of a sudden interested.

"He sure was, weren't you Daddy?" I emphasized Daddy so

they didn't still think I, a fifth grader, was married to a beer-swilling, ark-building child abuser.

I moved away from the crowd and as far from the cameras as I could get without returning home. I didn't like the lights, nor the questions. I didn't want fame. Not for this. Not for nothing.

But Daddy did. And if this don't explain what a bona fide psychopath my daddy is, then you ain't never gonna get it: He *liked* the idea that all these people thought he set a kid's house on fire, chopped him into pieces with God's own buzzsaw, and fed him to a gator the size of a crop duster. He even grinned while they was cuffing him. And the next day, his name was in everyone's mouth. Local. Regional. National. Just like Sluggo. Daddy got what he wanted. After all he put me through, I did that fucker a favor.

Miss Charlene was in the crowd, too, and I could feel her eyes burning through me. She pointed at me and stamped her cigarette out with her Reebok. My mind raced. I was afraid the jig was up.

She sauntered up alongside me, casual as all get-out.

"Good girl," she whispered. And no one heard it but me.

—End—

[1] It ain't like you're thinking with velvet drapes and a crystal ball. This sorceress worked out of her double-wide at the Scape Ore Swamp trailer park, where she also cut men's hair in her kitchen.

[2] He did not eat the crawdad with a stick.

[3] This is as bad as it sounds. After the first one hit my face, it broke my nose and two teeth. Then, the other one double bounced me right into that gardenia bush my momma watered with pickle juice. I know you're thinking this must be the incident that got him sober, but it wasn't and that's a whole other story for a whole other day.

[4] Ain't had one since. Never will again.

[5] In Podunk towns like mine it was perfectly normal for kids

whose feet reached the pedals to drive their drunk daddies around, so relax your sphincter, please.

[6] This is the universal sign for "Gun it, girl."

[7] He was full of ideas, but he spoke in a telepathic language I can't spell so you're going to have to trust me.

This story first appeared in Reckon Review.